Ada Buisson

THE BARON'S COFFIN
and Other Disquieting Tales

THIS IS A SNUGGLY BOOK

ISBN: 978-1-64525-108-8

The present text is based on the stories that were originally published in *Belgravia*; a number of amendments, however, have been made where obvious errors existed.

THE BARON'S COFFIN
and Other Disquieting Tales

Ada Buisson (1839–1866) was born in 1839 in Battersea, the daughter of merchant John Francis Buisson and Dorothy Jane Smither. In the 1850s, the family moved to Brighton. She published her novel *Put to the Test* (1865) with Maxwell which introduced her to Mary Elizabeth Braddon who later published several of her stories in *Belgravia*. Buisson died in 1866 in Boulogne-sur-Mer, France.

CONTENTS

THE BARON'S COFFIN
and Other Disquieting Tales

THE BARON'S COFFIN

CHAPTER I.
THE DISCOVERY.

DOWN in the south-west of France, not very far from Bourdeaux—or, to speak more exactly, about the middle of a line drawn directly from that town to Aire—stands a curious old château.

You might pass within a stone's-throw of it and not be aware of its existence, so closely is it shrouded by the thick forest of pines for which that part of the country is famed.

Its position is very solitary, far removed from even a village, and the little rutty road leading to it is but a cross and unfrequented cut from one highway to another. Still, there it stands under the blue skies of Gascony, surrounded by its dark woods; an enviable possession, in spite of its loneliness and queer architecture. And dark deeds were done there in times and by men not very long passed away.

I made my acquaintance with the place, under a professional introduction, in this wise: I was an architect, young, struggling; with, I thought, a great deal of talent, which society neglected to its own injury and mine. I had no work, and I had no means; moreover, I was in feeble health. One day my old master, who had always had a kindness for me, said, "Owen, my boy, I've got a job for you to do, if you are not too much engaged" (the dear old fellow spoke quite gravely, though he knew as well as I did that my only engagements were dinners and suppers with my fellow-idlers)— "to go abroad."

"I daresay I could manage it," I replied quickly.

"It's to go and examine an old château in the south of France—a tumble-down old place, I'm told, but which the family pride of its possessor won't allow to go to utter ruin. You've heard me speak of old Baron de Gaule? Well, it's one of his places; the one, I believe, from which his family derive their title; and though he hates his native country like the devil, he wants to take care of the old château. The job won't take you very long; but after you've made your report, he wants the place thoroughly repaired, or rather, restored. You can pass your summer weeks very pleasantly by taking up your lodging there and directing the work. You are to have English workmen sent to you. The old Baron would use English mortar, I believe, if he could. You speak French, I think?"

"Almost as well as English," I replied thankfully.

"Then the business is settled. I will give you the address of M. de Gaule, and you can take his directions from himself."

The Baron's directions were not much longer than my master's. "Only *restore* the place; add nothing, take away nothing, my good sir, and spare no expense."

In twenty-four hours after hearing those words I was on my way; in forty-eight hours I was standing within the pine-wood, looking up at the crazy curious old château, wondering whether successive generations had contrived this piece of architectural patchwork, or some clever but muddled brain.

Its only occupant was a tall, middle-aged woman, who to my eyes, unaccustomed to the dark beauty and picturesque costume of the southern women, offered a charming contrast to our English peasantry. She was prepared for my coming, and received me hospitably; not altogether sorry, I fancied, to have some break in her monotonous life, and some companion in her solitude; for I found she had been busily employed for my comfort, and was most courteous in her endeavours to smooth the way to conversation. Truth to tell, my French was not quite so perfect as I had first thought it. However, we soon became excellent friends; and though my conversation was confined to short phrases and pleasant grimaces, I soon learnt to understand her perfectly.

It was rather a dull life, when the novelty of the place and climate had worn off. My surveying, of course, occupied most of my mornings; but I had no intention of over-working myself, and it was difficult to find amusement for the leisure hours. I couldn't always be walking about the country; being companionless, it was slow work; neither could I be content to spend the long evenings smoking under the pines. Again, even Josette's conversation was apt to grow tiresome; and I had no books beyond those my profession required. I began to understand the word *ennui*, and to feel ungrateful to the old Baron for his job, and to pine for London smoke; when one morning Josette, to whom I had confided my disgust of life, said, in her most maternal tones, "Monsieur should distract his mind. Why doesn't monsieur read? Reading is very amusing."

I believe Josette thought she was introducing me to a new branch of education; she spoke the word "read" in so solemn a voice.

"And where shall I find books?" I asked impatiently.

"Surely monsieur knows; surely monsieur can get them for himself," Josette said nervously.

"He certainly could, if he knew where from," I answered pettishly.

"Why, in Monsieur le Baron's room there were books; numbers!"

"In the Baron's room? whereabouts?"

"Why, under the big bed."

And after saying that, Josette put the bottle of wine she was bringing me on the table, and went out of the room.

I finished my breakfast, and then went up slowly to the room called the Baron's. It was in a very out-of-the-way part of the house, low-ceilinged, octagon-shaped, and furnished with lumbering old furniture, after the bare fashion of old French châteaux. I had visited it but once or twice, my attention being still given to the more modern portion of the house. Evidently Josette held it in disfavour, for the dust lay thickly on chairs and tables, and on some of the furniture were large stains of mould; while over the closed windows spiders had woven curtains of delicate web. I threw open the jalousies and let in a little of the fresh air and morning sunshine; and as I did so, a rustling and then sweeping sound came from under the English four-post bed, which stood in gloomy grandeur in the corner of the room.

I was not of a nervous temperament, and that sound did not even startle me; but when, the next moment, I stooped and lifted up the moth-eaten hangings to search for the box of books, I certainly did start back with an exclamation of something more than surprise. Under the bed stood a large black coffin.

For an instant I felt inclined to get away as fast as I could. I turned sick; but, as I said before, I was not naturally nervous, and the feeling soon passed off. Besides, the sunshine was flooding the dusty old room, and from the window a peaceful scene of woods and fields and deep-blue sky was visible; and I hold that daylight and nature are powerful foes to fear and superstition.

I looked again. It was a coffin; of that there was no doubt. A large coffin too, covered with black velvet and studded with black nails, and the lid was lying on it; but it bore no plate or cross or ornament of any kind. A sudden idea crossed my mind,—it contained the books, perhaps; and so I put forth my hand bravely, and, using all my strength, drew it forward. There was something uncanny in the hollow sound made by the lid as it fell on the ground; but I would not be horrified, and with a brave hand I lifted up a large sheet of fine lawn neatly covering something, and then a yellow piece of linen, and then something that looked like a garment. Grave-clothes, I thought to myself; and then my fingers touched some hard substances—books, thank Heaven!

A few dusty ponderous volumes of Voltaire, Rousseau, and other philosophers of the same genus, I soon pulled forth to the light of day, which they had evidently not seen for years, so yellow were their pages; and then I found a cushion lining the bottom, and a little pillow on which was the visible impress of a human head and a stain or two of blood.

The sight of the books had reassured me; but that round scoop in the pillow and the stains gave me another uncomfortable thrill. I turned eagerly to the lid and examined it. It had been used; there were the holes of the screws, and one long rusty nail was still sticking firmly in it, whilst on the outside were marks of its having come in close contact with a clayey soil. It had a dreadfully earthy smell too.

I drew back with a faint shudder. After all, it was a gloomy object to find under that gloomy bed, in that ancient gloomy room; and Josette had been so eloquent during our solitary evenings with horrible stories of the De Gaules past and present, that I may be pardoned if, as I bent over this strange piece of lumber and heard shuffling footsteps coming faintly along the passage, I uttered a horrified cry.

The footsteps came nearer, and, it seemed to me, more rapidly, as my scream, or rather exclamation, sounded awfully audible through the stillness of the house, and then to my horror the door of the room was opened suddenly, and a face, that even now I can never think of without a shudder, peered through it.

It was old; so old that features bearing the stamp of seventy years would have seemed youthful beside it, drawn and puckered and shrunk till it scarcely looked human, while two red seams on either side of the mouth seemed to extend it from ear to ear in a perpetual ghastly grin. On the chin grew a scanty tuft of long white hairs, but the scalp was entirely bald; and to increase the horror of such an object, the left ear was gone, and the right so frightfully mutilated that it was only by the position I recognised what the hideous lump of flesh had been.

My first thought was, that before me stood the former occupant of the coffin, and all the stories of ghosts, vampires, dead men wandering about their old haunts, wronged spirits tormenting those who had wronged them, rushed to my mind with the terrible conviction that I was about to be forced to add myself to the number of their believers, when from that hideous mouth came the sound of a human voice.

"*Que faites, vous là?*" said the aged apparition tremulously.

I don't know exactly what I said or what I did; I have a faint recollection of pitching a volume of Rousseau at the spectre's head, and then rushing down the old staircase at a rate that was increased by hearing a peal of goblin laughter echo through the house.

Josette met me. "*Mais qu'est ce que c'est donc?*" she exclaimed in alarm. "Have you seen the ghost of old Monsieur le Baron?"

"I have seen an awful object," I answered breathlessly. "I have seen—"

"*Moi!*" exclaimed a voice on the staircase, and looking up, there we saw the hideous face grinning at us over the balustrades.

"*Ah, mon pauvre grandpère, c'est toi!*" said Josette composedly; then turning to me she laughed till the tears dimmed her black eyes.

I went out of the château in a huff, for I was young enough to resent being laughed at by a woman, even though that woman were an ignorant peasant; and I remained out until nearly dark.

When I returned to the château, I found my dinner comfortably prepared for me, and Josette in a repentant frame of mind. She did not make any allusion to the morning's adventure, but when she brought me in my dessert she said, with the gracious familiarity the French lower class so often assume with their superiors, that she and her grandfather were going to sit in the garden under the limes, and that if I would come and smoke my cigar, I should find it very pleasant; and, added Josette, her grandpapa would be so glad to have a little talk, and he did not look so ugly in the dusk.

I was not altogether pleased with the invitation, but I could not do otherwise than accept it. The old man received me very politely; he was sitting in an arm-chair, placed so that the moonlight did not fall on his ghastly features. We made a few observations on the scene, on my object in coming to the château, &c.; and then the old man, keeping his hands curled in a curious fashion over the places where his ears ought to have been—I suppose to supply their lost assistance—said,

"I am sorry I frightened monsieur this morning. I know I am a frightful object to look upon; but at a hundred years of age one can't expect to be handsome."

"A hundred years! Are you really as old as that?"

"*Mais oui, monsieur*. It's a long life—a very long life; and the times I have passed through have been stirring times for France and Frenchmen: but I'm getting weary of it. Why, monsieur, my playmates were those whose bones are buried in heaps at Marengo and Austerlitz, who lie deep down in the blood-pits of the guillotine. I don't wonder you took me for a ghost; why, mine ought to be wandering about with the old Baron's; we've played together in life many a time." The old man's voice trembled more as he spoke the last words.

"The old Baron!" I exclaimed; "that is the father of the present M. de Gaule, I suppose?

Why, what makes his ghost walk more than the other De Gaules'; was he more wicked? Ah, and perhaps you can tell me for what reason he kept that ugly great coffin under his bed?"

"The coffin? Ah, the great black coffin!" repeated the old man slowly. "I remember that time well."

"Tell us, grandfather," said Josette. "It's a beautiful night to tell a story in the open air. Wait, and I'll give you a *goutte* to brighten your memory. There! Now tell us about the black coffin under the Baron's bed!"

CHAPTER II.
THE FAMILY FEUD.

I won't tell you, monsieur (began the old man), about the grandeur of the old château at one time, about the wealth and power of the De Gaules, and about their long history of wickedness. I daresay Josette has told you enough about all that; but you must try and bear it in mind, if you would understand the story of the old Baron's coffin.

It was about the year '94—a bloody time, monsieur, when those that deserved it and those that didn't met together at the guillotine;

when men were hunted about like wild-beasts by wild-beasts; when there was no peace or rest or safety in any corner of poor wretched France; when brothers turned against brothers, and parents feared their own children; it was in the very thick of those times that Monsieur Louis was Baron de Gaule. His father had died when he was but a child, and he came in to the money and estates when it would have been much better for him to have been still under the rod of the schoolmaster. He was a tall, fine man; not handsome, but of a figure that looked made for command. He liked commanding too, commanding not only the servants about him, but his equals, his brother and sisters, his friends and relations,—everybody about him. It was an unfortunate temper.

But in those times it was dangerous to displease the lower classes, and monsieur, as he was called—for he had dropped his title, like everybody else who cared for his head—had to restrain his temper at any rate towards his dependents. Perhaps that made him fiercer towards his brother and sisters. He certainly was a tyrant to them, especially to Monsieur Paul, and no one was much surprised when one morning M. Paul went off to Paris and joined the revolutionary party. He was a very handsome man, as different from his brother as day is from night; but though he had pleasant manners, and kind words for everyone, there was something in his eyes that told you the De Gaule wickedness had found a hiding-place somewhere about him. I don't believe he loved anyone, though he pretended to like his proud tyrannical brother, and to be sorry for his sisters. I don't believe he loved even pretty Ma'amselle Pauline, who almost broke her heart when he went away, and who was the only one of the De Gaules who will ever get into heaven, if what M. le Curé says is true.

From the time M. Paul went to Paris, a change came over monsieur,—he was gloomier than ever, but more civil to those about him, and he seemed to take greater interest in all the bloody work that was going on in the dreadful city.

Till that time the family, in spite of its rank and wealth, had fared well enough. They had been forced to yield up some of their property, but otherwise the Revolution had done them little injury. It is true, the family consisted of only the two brothers and their three sisters, and they all lived together in the quiet old château, far away from even a village;—but in those times seclusion did not insure safety.

Monsieur had always inclined to revolutionary principles; indeed, the De Gaules, even in the most flourishing times of the Bourbons, had never been famous for loyalty, and at the commencement of the Revolution he professed open republicanism. He contented himself with "professing," however, and abode quietly in his old château.

I've heard it said that M. Louis was learned; that he read enough to turn his brain; but I know that I never saw him with a book in his hand. He would stay for days in his room (that called the Baron's); but whenever I went in to attend him, he was either sitting gloomily in his chair, or standing staring out of the window; and though books lay scattered about the room, not one did I ever see him touch.

Well, monsieur, after M. Paul went to Paris, as I said before, Louis grew gloomier than ever; at first it was a quiet kind of gloom, then it became restless, and then anxious.

We all saw that; for M. Louis was the head of the family, the master of us all, in spite of the Revolution, and we used to watch him, and study his face and his temper as some people do a weather-glass; and somehow, when he looked pleased, the old château seemed gayer, and we were all happier; whilst if monsieur looked cross or sad, it was a dull time for us. After M. Paul went away, there was not a gleam of happiness on M. Louis's face from one end of the week to the other; first he shut himself up in his room, then he took to wandering about the house, coming down among us servants in the kitchen, and going to the rooms of the young ladies. He seemed to hate being alone, though when he was with anyone he never talked; and after that mood passed away, he took to riding about the country, visiting the villages and the nearest towns. Sometimes after these visits he would throw himself off his horse and come striding into the château, his breath coming in great gasps, and his eyes rolling fiercely as he looked round on all of us, and he would shout out the last news from Paris as if it were almost maddening him. Poor little Ma'amselle Pauline would creep up to him then and try to soothe him, but he would shake her off and drive her from him, though at other times he would speak to her more kindly than he ever spoke to any other human being. Those were wretched days indeed, monsieur.

One day I was helping in the kitchen (there were not many servants about the château in those times; besides, I was a clever cook, and could serve up a dinner which even M. Louis enjoyed), when I heard monsieur coming along the passage, clanging his spurs on the stones.

"There's no change for the better in his humour," I thought to myself as I listened; and I was right, for the next moment he put his fierce face into the room, and shouted to me to go to him, as if I were a dog and he my master.

"I suppose you'd be frightened to put your nose outside the gates!" he exclaimed scornfully. "You wouldn't have the courage to go to Bourdeaux!"

"To Bourdeaux, monsieur?" I replied in amazement. "Has monsieur any business for me to do there?"

Instead of replying, he fixed on me his stern eyes, as if he would read my very soul. But I bore it without shrinking; I knew I was a faithful servant, and not a coward. Then he stretched out his hand, and as he laid it on my shoulder I felt that it trembled like a child's.

"Antoine," he said, "I believe as far as men can be good and true in these God-deserted times you are. I am going to test your fidelity and friendship, and I vow that, if ever the life shall be spared me, I will repay you if you stand by me in this hour of trouble."

"Monsieur has only to say what he requires done," I answered quietly; "my family was always faithful to the De Gaules."

He put his arm through mine and led me out to the group of pines standing there just to the left of the château. Though the sunshine was pouring down like molten gold on the country all round, it was cool as an autumn evening under the shade of the wood; and monsieur seemed to grow calmer as we walked among the trees.

"It's the old story, Antoine," he began, after carefully looking round; "the old story of brotherly hatred and treachery."

I started. "Not M. Paul!" I exclaimed; for though I had always liked him better than M. Louis, I distrusted him, and always feared that some day the evil shining through his blue eyes would work its way out somehow.

"What!" said monsieur scornfully, "have you too been taken in by his false smiles? Perhaps you would rather serve him than me—would you? Speak quickly."

His fierceness came back again; he seized my arm, and, with another of those alarmed looks round him, put his other hand in his bosom as if in search of something.

"I serve the head of the family," I replied calmly. "I am the servant of the *Baron* de Gaule, not of M. Paul."

He looked at me again, and then dropping my arm, said:

"I will trust you; I *must* trust you. You know I can reward you if you are faithful, and I think you know my temper well enough to know also that I could and would revenge myself if betrayed."

I did indeed, and yet I did not shrink from him.

"I have heard from Paris," he said in a quieter tone, "that there is every reason to believe my brother is playing treacherously with me. He hates me, and wants the property; you can guess what he means to do."

"Denounce monsieur!" I whispered.

"I am told that there is someone waiting to see me at Bourdeaux who has a message for me from Paul—some overtures he wishes to make, I suppose; and I am further told that it will be the worse for me if I do not meet this messenger." Monsieur paused a moment, then he added, "Now, Antoine, if I go—"

"Monsieur must not go," I interrupted; "he must send me."

"You would not be afraid? Cities are not like the quiet country."

"Monsieur, Antoine Bouteiller never knew fear," I replied.

"I believe you," he exclaimed, " and that is more than I could say to any other man in the world. Antoine, I accept your service; give me your hand, and swear that, come what will, you will keep faith fast to me, and not be won over by the false smiles and promises of my brother Paul."

So, putting my hand in my master's, I swore as he desired. Remember, monsieur, that that hand was then the clean hand of a French nobleman; there was only honour in touching it *then*.

Chapter III.
The Message.

It was a long distance to Bourdeaux; the old sun-dial standing in the courtyard of the château marked scarcely noon, as, mounted on M. Louis's own horse, I began my journey, and it was not very far off midnight when I reached the city.

It was but feebly lighted by lamps in some of the principal streets, and had it not been for the bright moonlight pouring down on it and the broad Garonne, I should have had some difficulty in finding the particular spot where I was to meet M. Paul's messenger. I knew it was to be on the quay, but I could not help being a little startled when a tall man wrapped in a cloak came and laid his hand on my horse's bridle.

"*Vous, voilà!*" said a voice that, in spite of the folds of the cloak being drawn over his mouth, I recognised as M. Paul's. I saluted him immediately; and then for the first time he seemed to be aware that I was not his brother. He drew back, muttering something between his teeth.

"Monsieur Louis couldn't come," I said; "he was not well enough to bear the fatigue of such a ride; but he has sent me to hear the news of M. Paul."

"Ill!" exclaimed M. Paul with a low, cruel laugh; "ill to death, I suppose? Perhaps it would be better for him that it was so."

"I hope not, monsieur," I replied, as if I knew nothing about his hatred for his brother, and trying to talk in the same respectful but familiar way I was accustomed to do with M. Paul. "I hope there's no bad news for him— no bad news for the family."

M. Paul walked on beside my horse for a few minutes without speaking. At length he turned to me, and said in his own quiet voice, but anxiously, "It's not likely, Antoine, that I should be away from my post in Paris at this time, unless fears for my family induced me. I have some power with the party now paramount, but not sufficient to insure protection to a declared enemy of the Republic."

"M. Louis an enemy of the Republic!" I exclaimed; "why, there couldn't be a stancher supporter of it! He's as red a Republican as yourself, M. Paul!"

"Bah! my good friend, it's easy enough to lie in this world, but not so easy to make yourself believed," M. Paul replied, taking out a small pocket-book and beginning to scribble something in it as he walked. "Look here, Antoine, I daren't do more than this—I daren't say more; but the sooner my brother Louis gets out of France the better for him. Give him this paper, and tell him what I've told you. These are fearful times for us all; natural ties bind no more than wisps of straw. Some fiend is calling for blood, blood; and as long as one can save one's own self, one dare not deny that of one's kindred. Get back to the château, Antoine, as fast as you can, and do as I tell you; it's the best and only advice I can give. Good-night."

He stood there under the moonlight, saying that in his quiet voice, and looking so sad and anxious, that I could not but think he meant what he said, and that M. Louis's suspicious nature had led him to imagine evil. I touched my cap to him.

"If you would just say a word how to manage to get master away, monsieur,—I don't believe he will be persuaded."

"*Tant pis pour lui!*" he replied, moving off. "I have done what I can; good-night." And before I could say another word he was gone.

I was not much of a scholar, and turn about that little bit of paper M. Paul had given me as I would, I could not make out a single word. But I was fortunate enough to meet little Mademoiselle Pauline in the pine-wood, as about noon next day I rode into the château grounds. No one knew where I had been except M. Louis; but I suppose mademoiselle guessed there was something unusual stirring to occasion my long absence, and she was on the watch.

A sweeter, kinder-hearted little lady than Mademoiselle Pauline I never knew; she was the only good thing about that gloomy old place, for the other two young ladies were very much like their brothers in disposition; Mademoiselle Marie resembling M. Louis, and Mademoiselle Clotilde, M. Paul. Well, when she caught sight of me, she came running up, and catching hold of the horse's mane, she exclaimed,

"Where have you been, Antoine? Tell me at once; I know there is something wrong going on by Louis's face; tell me out truly and boldly, Antoine." And she tried to look commanding and stern like her brother, but couldn't, because she was terribly frightened.

"Ma'amselle," I said sorrowfully, "if you want to know your brother's secrets, you had better ask him. Will you be kind enough, to read this paper to me? it's a note I have just found on the road."

She took it and glanced at it, and then looking up at me, she cried,

"Antoine, do not lie! This is my brother Paul's writing; where did you get it?"

"Will ma'amselle read it to me?"

She bent her head over it, and her hand shook like an aspen-leaf.

"Things are looking black for you. The only plan I can think of is flight, or the one suggested. Should you determine on the former, let me know, and I will do all I can to delay a crisis."

We were neither of us great scholars, though ma'amselle could read beautifully, and when she looked up and asked me in a frightened tone what it meant, I could no more tell than she.

"Did Paul give it you?" she asked presently. "What! has he been so near without coming to see us, to see me?" and then she bent her poor tearful eyes again over the paper, and read once more.

"It's very dreadful," she said; "but do you know, Antoine, sometimes I think that—" She paused. "It's awful not to be able to trust one's own brother," she added. "Let us go to Louis."

Monsieur was in his room, standing staring out of the window, as was his habit. He let me come in, but ma'amselle remained at the door.

Then I told him about my meeting with M. Paul; and he gave a horrible smile as I told him how disappointed he seemed at finding it was not his brother; and he muttered, "I thought so—I thought as much." And then, catching hold of my arm, he cried loud enough for ma'amselle to hear, "Why didn't you shoot him dead where he stood? Traitor! You are all traitors together. To hold his life in your hand, when you knew it was a question between mine and his, and not take his! My God!"

And then he tore the paper from my hand, and almost hurled me out of the room; and there, as his sister and I stood in the passage, we could hear him raging within like a furious beast.

Ma'amselle Pauline put her hand on the balustrades, and crept downstairs; and then, as I followed her, she drew me into her own little room.

"Good kind Antoine!" she said, with her cheeks looking hot and red, and her eyes wild; "what shall we do? I believe he spoke truly: it must and will be his life or Paul's. They hate each other like wicked fiends instead of loving each other as brothers. What shall we do?"

"If Monsieur Louis would leave France," I began.

"He will never do that; he will stay and fight it out," she answered. "Why, Antoine, you have known Louis all his life, and can you remember a single instance of his giving way?"

I shook my head.

"Or of Paul being true?" she went on. "No, no, Antoine; the De Gaules have been a sinful race from the beginning, and in the end it will be the same. What shall we do, Antoine?"

Meanwhile, overhead we could hear the furious tread of M. Louis. It startled the poor young lady several times, and each time she exclaimed, "What shall we do?"

And then Mademoiselle Clotilde called her, and she was obliged to go away. There were so few servants in the château, the young ladies were obliged to do a great deal; and somehow it always seemed that Mademoiselle Pauline had the heaviest share of household work.

As she went away, she whispered, "Don't tell anyone, Antoine; and after dinner come into the great salon; I want to speak to you."

I never shall forget that dinner. I waited behind Mademoiselle Marie's chair, for M. Louis still remained in his room; and it was dreadful to watch the face of little Ma'amselle Pauline opposite. But she bore up bravely, ate and drank, and talked to her sisters as if her heart was the happiest in the world. Only once or twice, as she caught my eye, she gave a little start, when M. Louis's footsteps overhead frightened her.

Then I went to her in the great salon; but Mademoiselle Clotilde came too, and so I could get no more talk with her that night.

As for M. Louis, he went out as soon as the dusk had fallen, and did not return till dawn; and then, to judge by the sweat his horse was in, he must have ridden far and hard.

He looked frightfully haggard, and his eyes were fierce and bloodshot; but as I opened the great door to him, he said to me so gently, "Get to bed, Antoine," that I took courage to reply,

"I was in hopes, monsieur, that you'd gone for good."

"No, Antoine; I'll fight it out with him," he answered, but in a less ferocious tone than I had heard him use for a long time when speaking of his brother.

CHAPTER IV.
THE STRATAGEM.

How we watched the next day! Monsieur Louis from his window, I from mine, and little Ma'amselle Pauline from the flat roof of a part of the château, to which she had ascended through a small window in the roof. How we watched! How we listened to the slightest sound on the road! But the time rolled on; noon, afternoon, evening came, and there was no sign of soldiers near. The old château still stood peacefully among the unbroken stillness of the pine-woods.

M. Louis had been gloomier than ever all day; but to me and to Ma'amselle Pauline he spoke once or twice in an almost kind manner. He took nothing from dawn to dusk except a crust of bread and a large glass of brandy; and I observed that he scarcely ever moved from his standing position at the window. I had often seen him stern and unsociable, but never in such a mood before.

When it was quite dusk he roused himself a little, and then, precisely at nine o'clock, he put on a large cloak, and, calling me to follow him, set off at a rapid pace through the wildest and most secluded part of the grounds. We walked very fast, but it was dark when we reached the confines; and there, under a tree, I could dimly see the figures of two men, with some dark object lying at their feet.

My master walked on, and spoke for some minutes to these men; and then they went away, leaving the dark object on the ground.

Monsieur waited till they were out of sight, and then he called to me, and, pointing to the thing, said,

"Antoine, I want you to help me carry this."

It was a large black coffin.

"Is it heavy?" I asked, rather horrified, and raising up one end.

"Not so heavy as it will soon be," my master replied in his fierce voice. "Now then, move on!"

While he spoke he had lifted up the other end, and there we both stood in the dark night, with that hideous thing on our shoulders.

As we walked home, more slowly than we had come on account of our burden, fearful thoughts filled my mind. What could monsieur want a coffin for? Was there an occupant ready for it, or did he mean to commit suicide? The last surmise seemed scarcely probable; suicides seldom trouble themselves with funeral arrangements. When we reached the château, who should meet us, creeping out of the great salon, but Ma'amselle Pauline? She carried a candle in her hand, and I shall never forget her white scared face as she held it up and let its light fall on the great black coffin.

"What is it for?" she muttered between her clenched teeth. "O Louis, it is not Paul! Say it is not Paul!"

But Monsieur Louis only lowered the coffin from his shoulder, and, telling me to carry it up to his room, himself led the way.

Ma'amselle Pauline followed; and then, as we set our load down in the centre of the polished floor, she dropped into her brother's large chair, and exclaimed again, "O Louis, say it isn't Paul!"

He took no notice of her, but, taking the candle, knelt down by the coffin and began examining it carefully, and I did the same. There were small holes in the lid, and it was deeper than coffins usually are; whilst at the back there was a large air-hole, carefully concealed by the fringe of the lid. I began to understand its use, and so did Ma'amselle Pauline.

"Now then, Antoine, listen to me," monsieur said, as he looked up with horrible satisfaction from his examination. "I was not to be deceived by that kind advice to fly from France. I knew well enough what would happen; and I would rather face them all here with my sword in my hand, than be fired at in flight. If I should be arrested by order of the Convention, I also know my fate. This is what I propose doing: if strangers come to the château, you must give out that I am dead, and immediately close the coffin-lid on me and bury me in the vault in the chapel. If Paul comes with them, you need only place me in the coffin, and leave him and me to do the rest. You can let me stay safely in the vault for twelve hours; but after that, Antoine, Pauline, my blood will be upon your heads. There, now go; leave me alone, for God's sake!"

"I cannot, I cannot hear of such a dreadful, wicked thing!" Ma'amselle Pauline began, clasping her little white hands entreatingly. "O Louis, listen to me: hide while there is time—hide!"

"And what hiding-place within ten leagues of the château does not Paul know?" fiercely interrupted her brother.

"O Louis, he is not so bad!" mademoiselle said piteously. "Only try, and I will watch, and pray him—"

"Be silent, and go to bed. Do not preach to me; my mind is made up," monsieur answered sternly; and then he went out of the room; and as neither I nor the poor young lady liked to be alone with that hideous thing, we also went away to another part of the house.

"O, that these awful days were over!" ma'amselle murmured as she went into her own room.

But they were not over yet; they were only beginning.

The sun rose the next morning as bright and glowing as if it rose upon Paradise rather than great bloody France reeking like a slaughter-house. I could scarcely bear to look out on the brightness; still, it was some comfort to see that in the sunshine the country looked peaceful and quiet as usual; that between the trees there was no sign of glittering arms or terrible uniform.

I took a cup of coffee to monsieur's room as early as possible, but found him occupied in writing, and could not induce him to take it.

"Keep it for twenty-four hours hence, Antoine," he said; "I would dare wager I shall want it then. Remember, Antoine," he added, "*twelve hours* at farthest—for your life remember that!"

Monsieur looked at the black coffin lying at his feet as he spoke, and I shuddered.

Just then Ma'amselle Pauline called me softly; and when I went to her, she beckoned me to the window where she was standing.

"Look out to the west, Antoine; do you see anything?" she said, in a quiet, frightened tone.

I did look, and I saw a faint glittering far away along the Bourdeaux road.

"Mademoiselle, they are coming!" I said, feeling a great throb at my heart.

She grasped my hand, and away we both flew to M. Louis's room.

I think he had seen the glittering too, for we found him hastily arranging his room, shutting the jalousies, and giving it as much as possible the trim, tidy look of a death-room.

Then with trembling hands we arrayed him in the death-clothes, placed the coffin on the tressles in the centre of the floor, and him in it.

He had a small vial in his hand, and as he lay there his face looked so corpse-like, that I should scarcely have been afraid of M. Paul himself seeing it. Then, calling in the other young ladies, to whom mademoiselle had already explained the danger, I left the room to watch for the approach of the soldiers, and give the alarm whether M. Paul was with them or not.

I never shall forget the terrible anxiety of that watching. It seemed as if they would never come, and yet they were moving, moving, ever moving along the road.

Then I lost sight of them in the pine-wood, and that seemed an awful moment when I again saw them—yes, absolutely within the château grounds.

Was Monsieur Paul with them? I looked attentively. Yes, riding a little apart from the rest, there he was, not daring to look up with his traitor-eyes on the home of his ancestors.

I left the window, and flew rather than ran upstairs.

"Monsieur Paul *is* there!" I exclaimed, rushing into the room, and then with one hasty glance at the coffin—when I saw the occupant raise the vial to his lips—I ran downstairs to the courtyard, where the soldiers were already dismounting from their horses. As the captain called out for Citoyen Louis Gaule, and the rest began entering the house, M. Paul beckoned me aside, and whilst he pretended to follow them, whispered,

"Has he escaped? God grant that he has!"

"He has, monsieur," I answered solemnly; "he died not an hour ago by his own hand. Rest his soul!"

For an instant M. Paul started back in pale consternation; then he seized my arm, exclaiming,

"This is some trick! Louis is not the man to kill himself. Confess the truth, Antoine, and I will do what I can to keep up the deception." I was taken aback by his soft sad tone, but I happened to look up into his evil eyes at the moment—that was sufficient.

"Go and look at him, monsieur," I replied sadly; "you will not doubt then. And what could he do? it was only a choice of deaths. Poison is not worse than steel. But go and look at him."

"I will," answered M. Paul in a hard tone.

The old man's voice quivered as he came to this, and Josette was obliged to give him another rather large goutte.

I shall never forget the sickening terror (he went on presently) with which I followed the soldiers and that cruel man up the old staircase to the Baron's room. I have gone through many dangers to myself since then, but I never remember feeling such an agony of fear as I did on entering that room, where Ma'amselle Pauline was sitting like a pale ghost on the floor, and that group of wild-beasts were crowding round the coffin in the centre. I went to the opposite side to where M. Paul was standing, and then I peeped over the shoulders of one of those wretches into the coffin.

I started; there was M. Louis, lying not in that forced stillness which he had first assumed, but dead: he could not but be dead, so white, so utterly still, were his features, so motionless his body, so breathless, pulseless. And then I looked up into M. Paul's face.

He was regarding the corpse with a gaze that was almost fiendish. For a whole minute his eye watched the pale face with an intensity of attention that, had the life-blood been flowing in its uncovered temples, he must have discovered it. Then he stretched forth his hand and took up the dead man's arm; and for an instant it lay placidly in his fingers, and then dropped with a dull lifeless thud on the breast.

After that he turned away, and putting his arm through one of the officer's, drew him apart, and talked in a low grave tone with him for some minutes.

Would they be satisfied? Would they go now, and leave us in peace?

I caught little ma'amselle's eyes for a moment, and they seemed to be asking me that.

Then Monsieur Paul and the officer came back to the rest, and the captain told them that apparently their work was done for them, that they might go down and rest themselves; and after a few savage words they went, with their swords clanging down the great staircase,—a horrid sound; and Monsieur Paul, the captain, mademoiselle, and myself were left alone with the corpse.

M. Paul went and again bent over the coffin, and he heaved a great sigh and murmured,

"Poor Louis, if he had only been persuaded! Poor Louis!" and then the traitor stretched out his hand towards his little sister; but she shrank away, and hid her face with her cold fingers.

The captain meanwhile had been standing at the window, but he came back as he heard M. Paul's voice, and taking up the coffin-lid, said gruffly,

"Come, come, if you want us to help you with this, we must go to work at once."

And then M. Paul sighed again, and with a hand that trembled, but not from grief, took the lid and laid it on the coffin, and then two of the soldiers were called, and I was sent for tools, and in a terrible quarter of an hour, monsieur, we had screwed up a living man in that hideous coffin. As we finished, the captain said quickly,

"Now to the vault, and then to breakfast. You're master here now, Paul Gaule, and we shall expect good wine;" and then he laughed, and M. Paul smiled with his lips, but his evil blue eyes remained anxiously fixed on the coffin.

"Let them dig a grave under the lime-trees," he said calmly.

"Monsieur!" I exclaimed in terror. "There's the vault in the chapel. The De Gaules were always buried there."

"Paul!" murmured the poor young lady.

But he answered, "What, a suicide in the old vault! Let them dig a grave under the lime-trees."

"Dig the hard earth under this broiling sun?" laughed the captain; "why the men would throw him to the dogs first!"

M. Paul turned pale.

"Well, then, to the vault!" he exclaimed. And then the three soldiers helped me to lift up the coffin, and we bore M. Louis down out of the house, across the sunny courtyard, to the little chapel, which had not been opened for many a day; and M. Paul, with his own hands, helped to lift up the flagstone before the altar, and then, by the light of a single candle snatched from one of the candelabra, we lowered Baron Louis de Gaule among the remains of his ancestors. A living man among the dead!

And there we left him; and as M. Paul put the key of the chapel into his pocket and came out into the sunshine, he looked round at everything with a smile.

O monsieur, there were fiends in those days!

All that day, till set of sun, the old château rang with obscene merriment. The soldiers forced their way into the cellars and larder; and those who were not lying under the pines dead drunk ransacked the old château from roof to basement; then they lounged about the great saloon, smoking, and swearing, and drinking, and singing ribald songs; or hunted the young ladies from room to room, or insulted us servants; whilst M. Paul sat at a little table, in the shade there of those limes, with two or three of them, and sang republican songs; and kept shouting to me to bring wine, to supply his friends with wine, the best wine!

It seemed to me as if that great blazing sun would never go down; and yet the hours were rolling on, and if more than twelve passed whilst the Baron was in his living tomb, there would be blood on our heads,—on poor little ma'amselle's, who sat there still on the floor in the Baron's room, and on mine.

Chapter V.
The Result.

I cannot tell you the joy of my heart at, an hour before dark, seeing signs that those drunken wretches were about to depart. It wanted but half an hour of the twelve that M. Louis might safely remain in the vault; and Ma'amselle Pauline, having come down from the room, stood in the dark shadow cast by the little chapel, waiting for me.

I counted each minute as it passed, and there they rolled on, and those wretches still lingered by their horses and wouldn't mount. My God! that was the most terrible half-hour I have ever passed.

Mademoiselle was standing leaning against the hard wall of the chapel, and wearying Heaven with her prayers; but Heaven was obdurate. Ten o'clock struck, and they were still shouting with their drunken voices in the château grounds.

I grew desperate, and in my desperation a thought flashed across my mind, the window over the altar! why not reach my unfortunate master by that? I fetched a flask of brandy, some tools, and a small pistol, and then, accompanied by my young lady, I crept quietly round to the back of the chapel.

There was a tree growing tolerably near; with a little exertion I soon reached the window.

"Holy Mary grant you may not be too late!" whispered mademoiselle. And then I opened the window gently, and let myself down on to the ground behind the altar.

I was not nervous naturally; but still, there was something awful in going down among the dead to wake up the living; and a cold sweat ran down my face as I moved gently towards the altar to get a candle before descending into the vault. But, to my surprise, the flagstone lying on the altar-steps nearly threw me down; and from the open vault came a faint light. Could the Baron have got out of the coffin?

Almost numb with a ghastly kind of terror, I reached the edge, then down a ladder placed there into the vault. At the farther end, where the coffin had been deposited, stood a man, stooping down and watching something. Tools were scattered about, and the lid of the coffin was standing against the wall. I made no noise. I did not see the man's face; but I knew it was M. Paul.

"Now," I thought, "as M. Louis said himself, it is but a question between their two lives." So I raised my pistol, and pointed it at the stooping figure; just then a feeble groan echoed through the vault, and I fired. A maddening moment followed. I saw a man turn on me like an enraged beast, and as we closed together in a struggle that was to be death to one of us, I caught sight of a ghastly face rising from the coffin.

Then, monsieur, whether I fainted, or became insensible from a blow, I am not certain, but it was dark for a long time.

I woke up lying on my back in the cool night-air, with the stars of heaven peeping at me through the trees. Beside me was a tall figure partially dressed in white, partially naked, busily employed in digging. The hideous reality came back to me at once. But was it M. Louis or M. Paul? Which life was gone?

I rose up faintly, and looked around; beside me lay the black coffin with the lid covering it, and the moonlight was playing on the white features of the Baron Louis digging in the earth. As I rose up, M. Louis came up to me.

"We must make haste," he said, "and bury it out of sight. They'll be back again before dawn."

He spoke huskily, and not altogether like a rational being; whilst his features were awful to look on.

"Where is Monsieur Paul?" I asked in a low voice.

"Dead," he answered; "in there;" and he pointed to the coffin. "Come and dig; I tell you they'll be back before dawn."

And I did dig; and the black coffin lay there beside us.

"Did you kill him?" I asked presently.

"Dig," said the Baron; "they'll be back, I tell you."

There was a faint glimmer of dawn in the eastern sky when that grave was finished, and then I had to go into the chapel for ropes to lower the coffin into it.

On the altar-steps sat Ma'amselle Pauline. How she had got there, I do not know. She did not speak a word as I entered; she did not even raise her eyes from the gaping vault at her feet, but sat like one in a trance.

I returned to M. Louis, and together we lowered the coffin into the grave, and shovelled in the earth.

"We must make it flat, we must make it flat!" the Baron shouted as he jumped into the grave from time to time, and trod down the earth with his feet. "Flat! flat! that they may not discover it."

He looked so awful, so fiendish, almost dancing there on his brother's corpse, that at length I could stand the sight no longer, and I rushed into the chapel. The dawn was just struggling in through the open window, and its light fell on the poor young lady's bowed head. I went up to her and tried to speak, but my tongue would not utter a sound; I was dumb as the dead. And there she sat and I stood, while outside we could hear that husky voice shouting "Flat! flat!" Presently he came after me, calling my name; and then, as the gray light fell on his dreadful face and figure, and his sister saw him, she started up like one awakened from a dead sleep. "O," she exclaimed; "Louis, where is he?" and then she seemed suddenly to remember something; she shrieked out, "Buried alive! buried alive!" and she fell down like a stone at her brother's feet.

And those words of hers, monsieur, brought a terrible fear on me—one that, as I hope for pardon, never had crossed my mind before.

I staggered like a drunken man, and was about to rush back to the grave, when the maniac caught hold of me and flung me down into the vault, and there, as I struggled in the darkness, I heard the flagstone thrown over it.

[The centenarian paused as he came to this, and stretched out his trembling hand towards the brandy-bottle.]

The horrors of that night, monsieur, you must think will never end; and I thought the same. It was terrible to lie there among the dead, and fancy you could hear the muffled cries of a man reaching you through a wall of earth. If ever I got out of the place, I knew it would be too late to save him. The deed was done. It had been a struggle between their two lives, and Louis had won. I lay there for hours; it seemed to me ages; and then, to my intense joy, I heard footsteps overhead, and a gleam of light came struggling down, and a flood of light—for so it seemed to my eyes wearied from the darkness—and women's voices called my name. I contrived to crawl out somehow, and then I found Mademoiselles Marie and Clotilde, one holding brandy, and the other bread, and both pale as death.

It was evening, they told me. Their brother Louis had ordered them to wait until sunset before they released me. He had set off to Orleans, they believed; at any rate, he was gone; and Pauline was lying upstairs in a terrible fever, shouting out, "Buried alive! buried alive!" they supposed in fear for me.

I let them think so. I knew it was too late to do any good.

I went upstairs, dressed myself, and ate, and put things straight a little after the drunken revels of the soldiers; and when it was dark I took my spade and crept out to that dreadful place under the lime-trees. It was sickening work; and when I came to the black coffin, I dropped my spade and felt I could do no more.

No sound came from it. I took out my chisel, and set to work to take the lid off, but it was firmly screwed on, and I had to work hard for many minutes. At length it was off, and then, holding my breath with fear, I looked in.

It was a ghastly sight, monsieur. A face agonised and blackened, with staring blue eyes, the forehead bruised and battered, and the teeth clenched, absolutely closing in the nether lip; hands grasping each other with such force that one or two fingers were quite crushed. There was no doubt of what death he had died.

Years and years passed away after that. The old château was closed, for M. Louis went to Paris and showed that he was as stanch a republican as M. Paul had been. I followed him; and more than once, as I have heard of his ferocity and seen his white savage face, I have felt certain that it was some fiend who took possession of the body of the Baron when he rose from the dead that night, and that it was not my old master—bad as he had been—who did that awful deed.

As for the young ladies, Marie and Clotilde went to Italy, and took up their abode in some convent; poor little ma'amselle died of the fever; and well it was so, for she would have had a cruel life, haunted by the remembrance of that night.

When times grew more settled, M. Louis, or Baron de Gaule as he then dared to call himself, went to England, and married an English lady, the mother of the present Baron, and there he lived till, I suppose inspired by a love of country, he returned to the château for a few months' visit, and died suddenly.

He never forgot his promise to me, and not only gave me money whilst living, but provided for me in his will.

But we rarely met; I think even his heartlessness could not bear the sight of me. He saw no priest; and I believe the story of that awful night—of how he got his brother into the coffin, of how he overowered him, or even of how he himself contrived to revive from that deathlike trance-never passed his lips. He died as he had lived- gloomy and unrepentant. The only allusion he ever made to the past was on the evening of his death.

"Antoine," he said, "under my bed you will find the black coffin—don't bury me in that. Remember, I won't be buried in that I could not rest."

And after his death, to my surprise, I found that coffin, empty too, under the bed in his room. It looked strangely new, considering it had been buried in the earth for, I thought, years and years.

How it was, how it got there, what became of the remains of M. Paul, I cannot tell you. There lies the ugly thing as you saw it, after having been buried twice, and having twice mysteriously got rid of its occupant, ready for a third; and a third, monsieur, will soon be ready for it, or rather, for one of its relations, for, like the old Baron, I don't believe I could rest in *it*.

Shall we go into the château, monsieur? The air blows somewhat keenly.

I rose up rather reluctant to enter the gloomy old place; but old Antoine put his arm through mine and led me in.

"Those times are passed and gone," he said; "and thank the good God they are. Ah, monsieur, if you like to hear stories, I can tell you many a one of those times, that while you hear shall make you forget your *ennui*. I can tell you something about myself which would make your flesh creep;—tell you how I became the hideous object I am."

But I thought I had had enough horrors for some time; and I must confess that instead of reconciling me to my solitude, that story of the Baron's coffin made me pine after my London home more than ever. It was with the greatest satisfaction that I received a letter from my employer, saying that he had changed his mind concerning the restoration of the old château, and he intended to employ the money in building a gothic villa on the banks of the Thames instead, of which he hoped I would immediately set about drawing the plans.

And so, in spite of the shady delicious old pine-woods, and the sunny blue skies of Gascony, I was very glad to turn my back on the old château.

THE GHOST'S SUMMONS

"WANTED, sir—a patient."

It was in the early days of my professional career, when patients were scarce and fees scarcer; and though I was in the act of sitting down to my chop, and had promised! myself a glass of steaming punch afterwards, in honour of the Christmas season, I hurried instantly into my surgery.

I entered briskly; but no sooner did I catch sight of the figure standing leaning against the counter than I started back with a strange feeling of horror which for the life of me I could not comprehend.

Never shall I forget the ghastliness of that face—the white horror stamped upon every feature—the agony which seemed to sink the very eyes beneath the contracted brows; it was awful to me to behold, accustomed as I was to scenes of terror.

"You seek advice," I began, with some hesitation.

"No; I am not ill."

"You require then—"

"Hush!" he interrupted, approaching more nearly, and dropping his already low murmur to a mere whisper. "I believe you are not rich. Would you be willing to earn a thousand pounds?"

A thousand pounds! His words seemed to burn my very ears.

"I should be thankful, if I could do so honestly," I replied with dignity. "What is the service required of me?"

A peculiar look of intense horror passed over the white face before me; but the blue-black lips answered firmly, "To attend a death-bed."

"A thousand pounds to attend a death-bed! Where am I to go, then?—whose is it?"

"*Mine.*"

The voice in which this was said sounded so hollow and distant, that involuntarily I shrank back. "Yours! What nonsense! You are not a dying man. You are pale, but you appear perfectly healthy. You—"

"Hush!" he interrupted; "I know all this. You cannot be more convinced of my physical health than I am myself; yet I know that before

60

the clock tolls the first hour after midnight I shall be a dead man."

"But—"

He shuddered slightly; but stretching out his hand commandingly, motioned me to be silent. "I am but too well informed of what I affirm," he said quietly; "I have received a mysterious summons from the dead. No mortal aid can avail me. I am as doomed as the wretch on whom the judge has passed sentence. I do not come either to seek your advice or to argue the matter with you, but simply to buy your services. I offer you a thousand pounds to pass the night in my chamber, and witness the scene which takes place. The sum may appear to you extravagant. But I have no further need to count the cost of any gratification; and the spectacle you will have to witness is no common sight of horror."

The words, strange as they were, were spoken calmly enough; but as the last sentence dropped slowly from the livid lips, an expression of such wild horror again passed over the stranger's face, that, in spite of the immense fee, I hesitated to answer.

"You fear to trust to the promise of a dead man! See here, and be convinced," he exclaimed eagerly; and the next instant, on the counter between us lay a parchment document; and following the indication of that white muscular hand, I read the words, "And to Mr. Frederick Kead, of 14 High-street, Alton, I bequeath the sum of one thousand pounds for certain services rendered to me."

"I have had that will drawn up within the last twenty-four hours, and I signed it an hour ago, in the presence of competent witnesses. I am prepared, you see. Now, do you accept my offer, or not?"

My answer was to walk across the room and take down my hat, and then lock the door of the surgery communicating with the house.

It was a dark, icy-cold night, and somehow the courage and determination which the sight of my own name in connection with a thousand pounds had given me, flagged considerably as I found myself hurried along through the silent darkness by a man whose death-bed I was about to attend.

He was grimly silent; but as his hand touched mine, in spite of the frost, it felt like a burning coal.

On we went—tramp, tramp, through the snow—on, on, till even I grew weary, and at length on my appalled ear struck the chimes of a church-clock; whilst close at hand I distinguished the snowy hillocks of a churchyard.

Heavens! was this awful scene of which I was to be the witness to take place veritably amongst the dead?

"Eleven," groaned the doomed man. "Gracious God! but two hours more, and that ghostly messenger will bring the summons. Come, come; for mercy's sake, let us hasten."

There was but a short road separating us now from a wall which surrounded a large mansion, and along this we hastened until we reached a small door.

Passing through this, in a few minutes we were stealthily ascending the private staircase to a splendidly-furnished apartment, which left no doubt of the wealth of its owner.

All was intensely silent, however, through the house; and about this room in particular there was a stillness that, as I gazed around, struck me as almost ghastly.

My companion glanced at the clock on the mantel-shelf, and sank into a large chair by the side of the fire with a shudder. "Only an hour and a half longer," he muttered. "Great heaven! I thought I had more fortitude. This horror unmans me." Then, in a fiercer tone, and clutching my arm, he added, "Ha! you mock me, you think me mad; but wait till you see—wait till you see!"

I put my hand on his wrist; for there was now a fever in his sunken eyes which checked the superstitious chill which had been gathering over me, and made me hope that, after all, my first suspicion was correct, and that my patient was but the victim of some fearful hallucination.

"Mock you!" I answered soothingly. "Far from it; I sympathise intensely with you, and would do much to aid you. You require sleep. Lie down, and leave me to watch."

He groaned, but rose, and began throwing off his clothes; and, watching my opportunity, I slipped a sleeping-powder, which I had managed to put in my pocket before leaving the surgery, into the tumbler of claret that stood beside him.

The more I saw, the more I felt convinced that it was the nervous system of my patient which required my attention; and it was with sincere satisfaction I saw him drink the wine, and then stretch himself on the luxurious bed.

"Ha," thought I, as the clock struck twelve, and instead of a groan, the deep breathing of the sleeper sounded through the room; "you won't receive any summons to-night, and I may make myself comfortable."

Noiselessly, therefore, I replenished the fire, poured myself out a large glass of wine, and drawing the curtain so that the firelight should not disturb the sleeper, I put myself in a position to follow his example.

How long I slept I know not, but suddenly I aroused with a start and as ghostly a thrill of horror as ever I remember to have felt in my life.

Something—what, I knew not—seemed near, something nameless, but unutterably awful.

I gazed round.

The fire emitted a faint blue glow, just sufficient to enable me to see that the room was exactly the same as when I fell asleep, but that the long hand of the clock wanted but five minutes of the mysterious hour which was to be the death-moment of the "summoned" man!

Was there anything in it, then?—any truth in the strange story he had told?

The silence was intense.

I could not even hear a breath from the bed; and I was about to rise and approach, when again that awful horror seized me, and at the same moment my eye fell upon the mirror opposite the door, and I saw—

Great heaven! that awful Shape—that ghastly mockery of what had been humanity—was it really a messenger from the buried, quiet dead?

It stood there in visible death-clothes; but the awful face was ghastly with corruption, and the sunken eyes gleamed forth a green glassy glare which seemed a veritable blast from the infernal fires below.

To move or utter a sound in that hideous presence was impossible; and like a statue I sat and saw that horrid Shape move slowly towards the bed.

What was the awful scene enacted there, I know not. I heard nothing, except a low stifled agonised groan; and I saw the shadow of that ghastly messenger bending over the bed.

Whether it was some dreadful but wordless sentence its breathless lips conveyed as it stood there, I know not; but for an instant the shadow of a claw-like hand, from which the third finger was missing, appeared extended over the doomed man's head; and then, as the clock struck one clear silvery stroke, it fell, and a wild shriek rang through the room—a death-shriek.

I am not given to fainting, but I certainly confess that the next ten minutes of my existence was a cold blank; and even when I did manage to stagger to my feet, I gazed round, vainly endeavouring to understand the chilly horror which still possessed me.

Thank God! the room was rid of that awful presence—I saw that; so, gulping down some wine, I lighted a wax-taper and staggered towards the bed. Ah, how I prayed that, after all, I might have been dreaming, and that my own excited imagination had but conjured up some hideous memory of the dissecting-room!

But one glance was sufficient to answer that.

No! The summons had indeed been given and answered.

I flashed the light over the dead face, swollen, convulsed still with the death-agony; but suddenly I shrank back.

Even as I gazed, the expression of the face seemed to change: the blackness faded into a deathly whiteness; the convulsed features relaxed, and, even as if the victim of that dread apparition still lived, a sad solemn smile stole over the pale lips.

I was intensely horrified, but still I retained sufficient self-consciousness to be struck professionally by such a phenomenon.

Surely there was something more than supernatural agency in all this?

Again I scrutinised the dead face, and even the throat and chest; but, with the exception of a tiny pimple on one temple beneath a cluster of hair, not a mark appeared. To look at the corpse, one would have believed that this man had indeed died by the visitation of God, peacefully, whilst sleeping.

How long I stood there I know not, but time enough to gather my scattered senses and to reflect that, all things considered, my own position would be very unpleasant if I was found thus unexpectedly in the room of the mysteriously dead man.

So, as noiselessly as I could, I made my way out of the house. No one met me on the private staircase; the little door opening into the road was easily unfastened; and thankful indeed was I to feel again the fresh wintry air as I hurried along that road by the churchyard.

There was a magnificent funeral soon in that church; and it was said that the young widow of the buried man was inconsolable; and then rumours got abroad of a horrible apparition which had been seen on the night of the death; and it was whispered the young widow was terrified, and insisted upon leaving her splendid mansion.

I was too mystified with the whole affair to risk my reputation by saying what I knew, and I should have allowed my share in it to remain for ever buried in oblivion, had I not suddenly heard that the widow, objecting to many of the legacies in the last will of her husband, intended to dispute it on the score of insanity, and then there gradually arose the rumour of his belief in having received a mysterious summons.

On this I went to the lawyer, and sent a message to the lady, that, as the *last person* who had attended her husband, I undertook to prove his sanity; and I besought her to grant me an interview, in which I would relate as strange and horrible a story as ear had ever heard. The same evening I received an invitation to go to the mansion. I was ushered immediately into a splendid room, and there, standing before the fire, was the most dazzlingly beautiful young creature I had ever seen.

She was very small, but exquisitely made; had it not been for the dignity of her carriage, I should have believed her a mere child. With a stately bow she advanced, but did not speak.

"I come on a strange and painful errand," I began, and then I started, for I happened to glance full into her eyes, and from them down to the small right hand grasping the chair. The *wedding-ring* was on that hand!

"I conclude you are the Mr. Kead who requested permission to tell me some absurd ghost-story, and whom my late husband mentions here." And as she spoke she stretched out her left hand towards something—but what I knew not, for my eyes were fixed on that hand.

Horror! White and delicate it might be, but it was shaped like a claw, and the third finger was missing!

One sentence was enough after that. "Madam, all I can tell you is, that the ghost who summoned your husband was marked by a singular deformity. The third finger of the left hand was missing," I said sternly; and the next instant I had left that beautiful sinful presence.

That will was never disputed. The next morning, too, I received a check for a thousand pounds; and the next news I heard of the widow was, that she had herself seen that awful apparition, and had left the mansion immediately.

A STORY TOLD IN A CHURCH

"WHAT shall we do? We are absolutely locked in. Every door is firmly closed, and I believe it is the doing of those dreadful boys, who have been trying to frighten us out of our wits all the afternoon with their ghost-stories." And Katie Bernard came laughing back to the spot where we were all standing and saying farewell words, after going through the pleasant labour of decking our little church with holly wreaths and shining laurel.

Katie was blessed with excellent nerves and a constitution that defied winter snows and summer heats, and I verily believe that she could have curled herself up in one of the great pews and slept the long night away as soundly as in her own white bed in the parsonage. But there were others amongst us (and I confess I was one of them) who already longed for the warmth of a fire, and who moreover began to find the glimmering of the white monuments and strange sculptured faces round about weird and a little ghostly.

"The dusk is falling. This is certainly most annoying," exclaimed Miss Montem, Ella Willis's governess, under whose charge we all were.

She turned a little pale as she spoke,—a rare thing for her; for a more self-possessed person than that handsome Miss Montem I never saw.

"What! are you, too, afraid of ghosts, Miss Montem?" laughed Katie. "Those boys will be delighted, then, at the success of their trick."

The governess turned almost scornfully. "I do not understand how one can fear that in which one does not believe," she said; "but I confess I have a particular dislike to remain in a church after dusk; it recalls to my mind the most painful story I ever heard." And then, turning hastily away, Miss Montem herself went and examined every door, even tried the vestry window.

Those "dreadful boys," however, had taken infinite care to bar every mode of exit; and even Dora Montem was obliged to admit that nothing could be done, but patiently to submit to imprisonment until our absence should cause anxiety at our various homes, and someone should be sent after us.

Meanwhile the twilight was momentarily deepening, and to my mind, at least, those half-wreathed pillars, those white faces peeping out from between the dark laurel, those stone figures on the two ancient tombs of Sir Guy and Sir Geoffrey Willis, lying with their legs crossed, began to look very eerie indeed.

We grouped ourselves about the seats in the chancel, and for a time talked and even laughed; but somehow, first one voice grew silent and then another, and at last those grim knights lying beside us were not more silent than we.

"Well, I must say this is a dismal way of spending Christmas eve," at length sighed Kate Bernard. "We ought to be round the fire now, roasting chestnuts and telling stories."

"Telling stories! ah, what a good idea! Why not amuse ourselves by that now?" exclaimed another voice. "Come, Ella, you have travelled; tell us some of your adventures."

"I? I never told a story in my life. No, ask Miss Montem; she has a gift for it."

The governess had been sitting a little apart from us, closer to the tombs than we cared to go; but as Ella spoke she raised her face, which she had been leaning on her hands, and even in the fading light I saw that she was deadly pale.

"I could not tell a story here," she murmured, "unless—would you like to hear the one of which I just now spoke? It is a terribly painful one, an awful one, but—"

There was a universal interruption of "Never mind. Yes, yes. Tell us that, Miss Montem."

We all knew the strange power the usually silent governess possessed for story-telling. It was the only time indeed she unbent or seemed like other human beings; but when she did condescend to indulge us, she possessed a fascination which none of us could resist; and we all knew that whilst listening to her we should care very little for the cold or darkness.

This was the story she told us:

Ten years ago I was seventeen, and serving my first year as governess-pupil at Mrs. Morris's school near Chichester.

No, Ella, you need not look pityingly at me, for I was very happy. Mrs. Morris treated me kindly and fairly; and amongst the girls I had friends whom I loved dearly. Besides,

Mount Silver, as the place was called, was conducted on the home principle, and there was not one of us who regarded our existence whilst there but as intensely satisfactory and enjoyable.

You may imagine that Mrs. Morris could not have been a very rigid schoolmistress when I tell you that we even received the news that we should be obliged to spend Christmas-day under her roof with no greater regret than one naturally feels when one finds the pleasure of seeing dear friends suddenly deferred.

The Christmas of ten years ago was the snowiest I remember. Roads were blocked up; even railways were subject to constant stoppages; and it happened that in our part of the country a small river had been so swelled by the snow as to have laid the surrounding ways under water. So, what with one thing and another, Mount Silver lay separated from Chichester, with almost as many difficulties to be overcome in a distance of twenty miles as if a hemisphere was between them.

Most of us were London girls, and the railway being unreachable, our fate was quickly settled. The only two who remained voluntary prisoners were Millicent Power and her cousin Irena Dupont.

Milly Power was the niece of the lady of the manor, Lady Jane Power, who, it was believed, intended to make her her heiress; and her home lay but a couple of miles from Mount Silver. But Christmas or any other "mass" was so dull with Lady Jane, who passed her time nursing her cat, knitting, and physicking her various imaginary ailments, that both Milly and Irena no sooner heard that the rest of us would be forced to spend part of the holiday at school, than they begged Mrs. Morris to allow them to do the same.

I think we were all glad that they did not desert us, though, perhaps, had—but I must not anticipate. They were our head girls, our leaders—Milly Power by right of age and rank, Irena Dupont by right of her daring spirit and rich beauty. Ah, heavens! how beautiful that girl was! I see her before me now, with her dark glowing eyes, her oval face, the rich Southern blood mantling her cheek with every emotion; so fresh; so eager in her enjoyment of her young life and splendid health.

She was cousin to Millicent by the mother's side; but, though daughters of two sisters, there was not a shadow of resemblance either in character or feature between them.

Millicent was fair, cold, haughty, proud of her ancient family—a little proud, I sometimes thought, of having money always at her command, and being the heiress of her aunt. But *I* ought not to make her any reproach, for she was a kind friend to me, and it was thanks to Milly's purse that my poor wardrobe could boast anything beyond the very humblest attire.

How it was that Irena Dupont lived also under the protection of Lady Jane I never rightly understood. She was not a penniless orphan, I knew, for she often alluded to her father and his vineyards down in the south of France; but yet she appeared to be in a great measure dependent on Lady Jane, and once or twice I noticed that she gave way to Millicent, proudly, but in a manner that betrayed she had a reason for so doing.

Were they fond of each other, those two cousins? Ah, that was a question which none of us could satisfactorily answer then—not even I, who was Milly's bosom friend.

They sang together sweetly, rode together; but never by any chance were they known to talk together beyond joining in ordinary conversation, and never did I see Irena give Milly one of those gushing kisses which she bestowed so liberally and gracefully on those she loved amongst us.

It was not, however, till the Christmas I am speaking of that I knew the great obstacle between them to be Milly's jealousy of her cousin's beauty.

We were sitting in the school room after tea, as merry a party as could be, in spite of our imprisonment, when Mrs. Morris entered rather abruptly, and with not an altogether satisfied expression of countenance.

"Millicent, my dear, I want you in the drawing-room," she said, slowly shutting the door. "Your cousin, Arthur Power, has ridden over perfectly desperate at finding the Manor House only presided over by Lady Jane; and he declares that the cold is so intense he really can't face it again to-night, and give him shelter I must. Most improper of him to come to a school for young ladies, I am sure!"

Millicent's fair face flushed, and a peculiar half-vexed smile curved her lips.

"Just like Arthur—he is so inconsiderate," she exclaimed, rising with her work in her hand.

"He wanted to come down here, but I would not allow that."

"Of course not," said Milly, walking rather hastily towards the door.

"Ah, Irena, you may as well come too. I—"

But Millicent turned almost abruptly, and with a strange forgetfulness of the respect she usually paid Mrs. Morris, exclaimed: "What for? Arthur is my cousin, not Irena's. She does not know him even."

Irena had risen, and was following, but at those words she dropped back into her corner by the fire, and a smile, half angry, half scornful, passed over her beautiful face. "True," she said quietly.

Mrs. Morris looked a little puzzled, but even she sometimes gave way to Miss Power; and so, without further remark, she linked her arm in Milly's, and they left the schoolroom.

We were not so discreet as our governess, however; and no sooner had the door closed than there was a general exclamation against Millicent, for Irena was the idol of the school; and then the French girl for an instant seemed to forget the restraint she had always imposed on herself, and lifting up her flushed face, with its rich, angry, glowing eyes, she exclaimed: "Nonsense! You forget Millicent is almost engaged to her cousin Arthur. It was natural she should wish to see him alone."

"Or natural, you mean, that she should not wish him to see you," exclaimed someone.

But if that was Millicent's wish, she was cruelly disappointed. Mrs. Morris, anxious to make up in some measure for our disappointment, had invited the doctor's and lawyer's families, living in the village close by, with the vicar's nieces, to come and celebrate Christmas-eve in the good old-fashioned manner; and no sooner did Arthur hear of the "party," than he invited himself to remain for it; and not all Mrs. Morris's hints at impropriety and inconvenience could induce the handsome young officer to dislodge himself.

To the excellent lady's intense relief, Mr. Power was a fashionably late riser, and she contrived to despatch us all the next morning to the church which we were to assist in decorating before he made his appearance; and I firmly believe, as she watched us all pass out of the garden gate, she thought she had manoeuvred skilfully past all danger until at least the evening.

School-girls of seventeen and eighteen are apt to talk a good deal on those subjects which good Mrs. Morris dreaded so; but I don't think my mind was ever much given that way, and Arthur Power certainly never crossed my thoughts when once I found myself in that ancient church, with holly and laurel wreaths, waiting to do justice to all the artistic taste we could muster among us.

We were soon scattered over the church, which was a singularly beautiful one, though centuries old, it having belonged to a wealthy monastery; and as usual Milly and I worked together.

She was not in a talkative humour, and so we spoke little except about the work; and when she suddenly left me, saying she must have a little exercise to warm her, I scarcely missed her.

Alas, that she ever took that ramble!

She was not gone long, and when she returned she was out of breath. "What do you think, Dora, I have found," she began; and then suddenly she paused and looked sharply round, for a man's laugh sounded from the chancel. "That's Arthur; let us go and see," she exclaimed.

And we did go, and what we saw was beautiful—Irena mounted on a chair, twining a holly wreath round a cherub's head; and there beside her, gazing up and handing sprays of shining green, stood Arthur Power. Two other girls were near, but it was Irena Dupont on whom those handsome blue eyes were fixed so earnestly that even our approach was unnoticed.

"So you have found us out, Arthur, in spite of Mrs. Morris," Milly exclaimed, with a smile on her lips, but O, such wildly angry eyes!

He turned immediately and held out his hand.

"Of course; you know I always manage for myself."

"So it seems, even your introductions."

"As to that, Miss Dupont is a kind of cousin, you know, and therefore an introduction was unnecessary; besides, I am making myself so decidedly useful, that even if I have offended against the *convenances*, I ought to be forgiven."

"And so you shall be if you will mount and finish this for me," interrupted Irena; and before even he could reply, she had jumped lightly down from the chair and joined another group of workers at the other end of the church.

Arthur turned and looked after her rather dolefully, and Milly's eyes flashed.

Ah, Heaven! how well I remember that Christmas eve! How joyously it began how gay we were! I know I can say for myself that never since have I laughed with such free-hearted joy as I did that night. There was little ceremony, no elaborate toilettes; we all knew each other, and the female element considerably preponderated; but the dancing was no less delightful, the smiles no less radiant, the enjoyment no less intense.

In the early part of the evening perhaps there might have been a little jealousy regarding the attentions of Arthur Power; but he soon showed such evident preference for Irena Dupont, that the rest retired from the contest.

And who could wonder that she should be preferred? Simply dressed in white muslin, with a sash of scarlet silk round her waist, Irena seemed to float amongst us like some goddess amongst her attendant nymphs. She never seemed to try to be dignified, and yet she always walked like a young queen, always stood amongst us with her tall graceful form as superior to the rest of us as Diana amongst her nymphs.

It was no use Millicent Power looking cold and haughty; Arthur cared not: he saw only those sweet dark eyes of her French cousin, heard only that rich merry laugh, cared only to wind his arm round that pliant waist.

Even in the games which relieved the dance, Arthur contrived always to be near Irena; and though now and then he paid attention to his cousin Milly, even she saw that it was because he felt it a duty rather than because he wished to do so.

I thought I knew Millicent Power well; I thought I understood her reserved character; but that night she puzzled me. She was too lady-like to show temper or even jealousy at Arthur's sudden desertion, but now and then she glanced at that part of the room where he was with such wild pained eyes, now passionately angry, now sorrowful, that even I wondered she could so betray herself to him.

Still she did not keep herself away from the rest; she joined in all the dances and games, and talked and laughed as excitedly as any of us. More so almost; and I recollect that it was Millicent's voice which was the first to accept the challenge that led to so much sorrow.

Our party was too large to be accommodated, even at the large school table, all at the same time, so we younger ones had taken our supper first and then returned to the dancing-room, leaving Mrs. Morris to entertain the elders; and so it happened that we had no wise friend near to prevent the commencement of as foolish a freak as ever wild young creatures planned.

How it was that the subject of ghosts was started I know not; but I remember that instead of returning to our games we stood grouped together listening to a wild story Arthur Power was telling; and though all laughed and declared their disbelief in it, there were few voices that responded to his challenge at the conclusion. "I would wager this," and he held up a small gold locket, "that not one person here would venture now to cross the churchyard alone, enter the church, and pass through and bring me a piece of the cypress waving over the broken tomb on the other side."

"What, make the tour of the churchyard in this cold! No thank you," said one sensibly.

"O, you may put on goloshes and a warm cloak; besides, it's a splendid night, the snow is hard as iron. Ha! ha! I see, ladies and gentlemen, it is the white feather, not the cold."

"I should not be afraid," exclaimed Millicent. "As you say, it is a splendid night: I will go."

"And so will I," I exclaimed.

"And so will I," said Irena.

No sooner said than done.

Upstairs we three adventurous ones crept to don warm cloaks; and then, cautiously opening the front door (for we knew if Mrs. Morris heard aught of such a proceeding she would quickly stop it), not five minutes later, I, with the key of the church in my hand, started at a quick pace over the hard snowy walk.

It was agreed that ten minutes after I had started, Millicent should follow, and at an equal period after Irena was to come; for, argued Arthur, the elders would probably have finished supper soon; and it would not be safe to wait for the return of each before the other started.

Ah, how well I remember that mad midnight walk! It was a brilliant night, but the cold was so intense that I had not reached the gate of the churchyard, close as it was, before I repented of my folly. However, I went in.

I was not of a timid nature; and that walk across the snowy church yard was not in the least fearful to me. The silence of the decorated ancient church, about which I had heard legends enough to terrify any one, affected me more; and I confess, as the door grated slowly on its hinges, I felt sorely tempted to turn and flee.

I did walk very quickly along the stone aisle; and it was with a gasp of intense relief that I stepped out into the snow and moonlight again through the little chancel-door, close to which stood the broken tomb and its dark cypress.

My hand trembled so, that I could scarcely pluck the bough; and then I fairly ran along the side-path which led to the other gate opening into the back garden of Mount Silver.

"By St. George, you have only been a quarter of an hour!" exclaimed Arthur Power. "I wonder how fast Milly will run. You look rather white, though, Miss Montem."

"The cold is intense," I answered rather crossly; "and it was a foolish thing to do."

"Did you meet the ghost of the monk?"

"Never mind whom I met; there is the cypress bough."

Arthur shrugged his shoulders and turned away, still watch in hand.

"Twenty minutes; no, twenty-five minutes. Milly must be having quite a gossip with the monk," he said presently, not quite so pleasantly though.

"Twenty-seven—ah, there she is!"

Yes, there was Milly, ghostly white and shivering.

Arthur approached her almost anxiously; and though he made some joking remark about her having met a legion of ghosts, I observed that he took her hand and began rubbing it, and then muttered something in a low tone, which, however, only turned Milly's shivering into a convulsive shudder.

"Give her something hot to drink," I exclaimed from my corner, where I was also still shivering. "The cold—no one knows what the cold of that church is."

And then Milly lifted up her eyes with a look. Heaven, how that look haunted me afterwards! And she managed to mutter with her sweet lips, "Yes; the awful cold."

"I wish to goodness Irena would come, now before Mrs. Morris returns," said someone. "She will be so angry about this;" and then Arthur Power looked at his watch again, but this time said nothing.

A silence fell upon us all; not a word was spoken; no one moved even; everyone listened—listened for that light step which should announce the approach for which somehow we all so longed.

The clock struck one; and again Arthur looked at his watch, and then again that silence continued unbroken; and there, motionless, we all remained waiting for her—for her who was *never to come to us!*

No use our listening; no use watching those slow-moving hands of the great clock—never, never more were we to hear the fall of those quick light feet. Time might come and time might go, but Irena Dupont would not return with it.

O, that miserable night! how the memory of it has haunted me! Those sad, horror-stricken faces, which not two hours ago had been so happy; the frightened whispering; the coming to and fro of anxious searchers waving their lurid torch light over the snow; the sobs, the tears, the wild hopes, and at length the blank despair—how I remember it all, as some dreadful confusion, which, strive as I would, I could not comprehend.

A mystery indeed had fallen upon us that Christmas night—a mystery which none could solve. All we knew was that Irena Dupont had gone out fresh and living into the snow and darkness, and that she never came back. The path from the house to the church was direct enough—it was perfectly safe; there were no bad characters about; so far as our human ken could reach it, all of us could declare to its perfect safety; and evidence of any struggle or accident there was none.

Search was not spared; and for weeks every means of discovering what had become of the lost girl was freely tried. But that solemn Christmas night refused to give up its secret; and the mystery of the beautiful French girl's fate remained still darkly hidden.

But, in spite of those great sorrows which come to disturb the current of life, commonplace daily realities must be thought of and faced. I had learnt that lesson in the year of hard struggling I went through on quitting Mrs. Morris's pleasant roof to take the place of junior teacher in a German school; and yet I confess I felt almost horrified at the contents of a letter I received one June morning from my old friend, Millicent Power.

She was going to be married to Arthur, she wrote, and she hoped I would come and act as bridesmaid. What! had she forgotten so soon that horrible Christmas story? I thought. With her usual forethought, she had enclosed a bank note for my travelling expenses; and she made her request in terms which a lonely orphan like myself was not likely to resist.

Lady Jane was dead, leaving Millicent sole heiress to her property; but Milly told me she could not endure the solitude of Power Place, and still lived with Mrs. Morris, from whose house she was to be married. I was to go to her there, and I should find more than one familiar face to welcome me.

It is only those who are homeless who can sympathise with me in the intense affection I bore to that dear old house and all its occupants, and the eagerness with which, in spite of my weariness, I leaned forward in the coach to catch the first glimpse of the tall, ivy-covered chimneys.

I knew the horn announcing the entrance of the coach into the village would be heard at Mount Silver, and I quite expected to see Milly's fair face at the garden-gate waiting for me. There was one figure standing there between the rose-bushes; but it was Mrs. Morris's, not Millicent's.

"No, my dear, I would not allow Milly out so late, though the evening is mild," she answered, after the first embraces were over: "her health is very delicate, and I sent her to bed."

Though Mrs. Morris spoke drily, and almost indifferently, I could detect anxiety in her eyes, and I knew that before long I should hear something of the reason; for I was a favourite of hers, and she had always treated me as a friend rather than a pupil.

I found that I was to sup in private with my former instructress; and I was scarcely surprised when, as soon as the first hospitable cares were over, she began abruptly, "Do you know, Dora, I am very uneasy about Milly? I am not at all sure that this marriage ought to take place."

I started.

"I mean, of course, on account of her health. Ever since that night when—when—you remember—Milly has been altering in a manner that perhaps others may not have observed, but which I have. There is a family malady hereditary to the Powers, you probably know—"

"Consumption! Ah, I have heard that."

"I wish it were only that," sternly replied Mrs. Morris, as if forcing herself to utter the words. "It is something more awful—insanity. Milly's nerves never seem to have recovered the shock of that dreadful night."

I was literally too horrified to say a word, and I knew scarcely whether to be glad or not when Mrs. Morris suddenly rose and proposed going to Millicent.

I was accustomed to her abrupt ways. Still, when she paused at Milly's door, and said in a sharp whisper, "There is a week still to the wedding—we must both watch and do our duty, Dora"—I shrank back in alarm.

And though that first interview relieved my mind, I had not been twenty-four hours constantly in Milly's company before I saw that Mrs. Morris's observations were correct: Milly was altered. She would suddenly break off in the middle of a sentence, even about Arthur, and fall into a stony kind of quietude, which was too strange to be the result of mere weakness. Sometimes, too, she was restless, and the anxiety for her wedding-day to arrive was incomprehensible and almost painful.

She could not endure solitude, either; and if by any chance she awoke from one of her frequent dozings and found herself alone, she would ring her bell with a fury which more than once broke the wire. Still she never permitted anyone to sleep in her room at night; and I was quite surprised when, the day before the wedding, she asked me if I would mind sleeping on the sofa at the foot of her bed.

Ah, that Sunday night was to be another of those which terror scorched into my memory!

It was an exceedingly hot night. The room was a large one, on the ground floor, and the open window looked into the garden. I could not sleep. Milly, too, tossed restlessly from side to side, and, though she slept, moaned piteously. Time seemed as if it would never move on, and hours seemed to elapse between the striking of each quarter. I suppose, however, I must have dozed, for suddenly I started up with the impression that someone had passed by me, and hastily looking towards Millicent's bed, I saw that it was empty

Why, instead of rushing to the door, I flung on a cloak, and, bare-footed as I was, darted through the French window into the garden, I know not—it must have been some fate that guided me, for there, dimly visible passing through the little gate into the churchyard, was a white figure. I flew along, but Millicent went faster than I, and with a strength and steadiness she never displayed in the day.

On she went—up the little side paths, never pausing, but going on swiftly, steadily, towards the chancel-door.

Surely now she must pause, unless by some chance the preparations for the marriage had caused the door to be left unlocked.

She passed in!

Ah, how I flew then, though why, except fearing some horrible catastrophe, I know not; and at length a second time I stood within that ancient church in the dead of night.

Even as I entered, a low piteous moan directed me to where I should follow my unfortunate friend; and there in one of the grim side-aisles, where the stone pavement still bore Latin inscriptions to departed monks, I saw that white figure kneeling and moaning and bruising her soft fingers against the hard stone.

"There—I know it is there," she muttered. "I lifted it then so easily, it must come up again. Don't shriek so, Irena—O, O, don't shriek so!"

And then, lifting up her white agonised face, she desisted from her awful scratching at the stone, and put her hands to her ears, as if to shut out some dismal sounds.

I stood transfixed with horror, not daring to approach, for I saw that though she had her eyes open she was asleep; but at that moment the chancel-door slammed. With an awful cry the sleeper started up, gazed wildly round, and then I saw her fall prone on the stone floor, the life-blood flowing from her lips.

There was no wedding the next day in that ancient church. Millicent Power lay gasping away her life, and murmuring only two words, "God forgive! God forgive!" But there was a horrified group standing round that stone and watching for the return of the explorer of the unknown ancient vault which was found under that cracked pavement. There was no need to make much inquiry as to whose remains those were which then were brought to the light of day—the long dark hair, a small ring, told all that was necessary to be told—Irena Dupont was found again!

But beyond those words which in her miserable sleep Millicent Power uttered, no light was shed on the mystery which enveloped her fate. I, who knew all that had passed, and had seen the wild agony of her face as she knelt and tore at the stones, felt that, unless insanity could be alleged in her excuse, Millicent Power's soul was loaded with an awful crime; and as I remembered how she had been walking in that aisle when she left me and returned uttering that exclamation which was never finished, I joined fervently in that dying prayer of hers, "God forgive."

That stone was broken in such a way that a chance glance would more likely have noticed that it could be raised easily than one accustomed to pass it day by day.

Probably she had raised it and discovered the vault, and leaving it open had forgotten it until that mad midnight visit. I had passed through the centre aisle; but Irena might easily have taken the side one, and—but enough of this—it is too dreadful, and—God forgive us all!

We were all huddled together as Miss Montem's voice dropped; and if there was a word murmured before we were silenced by the sound of steps without, it was only an echo of the prayer with which Dora Montem closed her story.

UNDER THE LILIES

WHEN I was sixteen years of age, I was sent for a couple of years' superior polishing to an establishment for young ladies kept by a very distinguished lady whom I will call Mrs. Furnival.

Many years have passed since then—so many, that I feel I may relate the following story with an easy conscience; for, painful and sad as it was, it has probably long since faded from the memory of all but the principal actors in it; and, dressed under new names, few will recognise it, and certainly none on whom it could have a damaging effect. Mrs. Furnival herself has been dead a long time, and the school has passed into other hands; so I think no one can reproach me with breach of confidence in telling the following history.

Mrs. Furnival prided herself on receiving pupils of the first-class only, and of educating them in such first-rate style as to render them polished ornaments of the most fashionable drawing-rooms on passing from her schoolrooms. The horror of her life was not ignorance, but *gaucherie;* the object of all her teaching not so much wisdom as elegance. To be awkward or vulgar was in Mrs. Furnival's eyes almost criminal.

We led easy lives at Maldon Lodge; for madame was consistent, and in educating us for luxury she taught us experimentally to enjoy it. We had maids to dress us, horses to ride; we dressed for dinner, and passed the evenings in the drawing-room, amusing ourselves with music and elegant fancy-work; we paid much attention to fashion and deportment, a degree less to accomplishments, and two or three less to general knowledge; and for all that our parents paid 200*l.* per annum.

The rules of the school were few and not very strict; the governesses were not very stern; and so it depended much on our own tastes and characters what kind of lives we led. For the industrious there were masters enough; for the idle, plenty of indulgence; the only things absolutely required were elegance, good manners, and a graceful carriage.

We naturally took kindly to life at Maldon Lodge, and I think there were none who looked forward with any eagerness to the time of leaving school.

A rebel, however, found her way into the orderly ranks of Mrs. Furnival's young ladies—a daring little rebel of seventeen, fresh from the wilds of Australia, the daughter of some distinguished person out there, and the heiress, we were told, of an almost fabulous fortune.

I remember her well, in spite of this lapse of years; I remember vividly every feature of her beautiful young face; I seem to see her before me again, with the ever-changing light in her glorious wild eyes, the rose-colour coming and going on her delicate cheeks, the sunlight losing itself in the rich red gold of her wavy hair. To look at her springing about in her daring disregard of all rule, grace in every movement; to listen to her sweet fresh voice singing in the very luxuriancc of gay-heartedness, who would have guessed the miserable future, or the doom hanging over her?

And yet, with all her airy loveliness, all her wild sweet grace, Myra Richardson won few hearts. She was my room-mate, and I was certainly the most affectionately-disposed towards her; nevertheless I never reached the point of loving her—I never felt my heart thoroughly warm towards her. There was something uncanny in her wild eyes, something that repulsed me in the tones of her voice, even in her quietest and most affectionate mood. Amongst the rest of the girls she was regarded with a mixed feeling of jealousy and wonder; jealousy of her wild beauty, wonder at her wild ways.

At first her peculiar manners were looked upon as the consequence of her colonial birth and education, and both governesses and pupils endeavoured by sneering allusions to tame her into a civilised kind of schoolgirl; but sneering allusions, as well as more open reproof, fell on a deaf ear, or one too careless to heed them; and after a six months' residence at Maldon Lodge, the little Australian was still as obstinately wild as one of the kangaroos of her native land.

This graceful savageness was, however, her chief fault; for she was clever, good-tempered, generous—indeed, possessing all those qualities calculated to win popularity, had they not been marred by her elfish instability of character. Instability of character as we thought! Ah, had it been only that!

It was a bright soft evening in early June—a Saturday, I recollect, for both Myra Richardson and myself had been spending the afternoon with my cousin, and we were sitting in Mrs. Furnival's library, where we had gone, as was customary, to report ourselves to the principal on our return, when the door was opened quickly, and the head-teacher entered.

Where is Mrs. Furnival?' she demanded sharply, and closing the door carefully behind her.

"We are waiting for her now," I answered, surprised at her abruptness, for Miss Morton was one of the slowest and most apathetic of creatures. "Is anything the matter?"

"Matter!" she repeated in an unusually sharp tone. "Only that the house has been *robbed,* and most mysteriously so, within the last hour."

"Robbed! What, in broad daylight? Impossible!" I exclaimed.

"If the principal had only been at home!' continued the teacher in the same anxious tone; "but now, of course, I am responsible. I was sitting in the room, too, but an hour ago correcting the first-class themes, and everything was quiet enough. I can't imagine how it happened."

Before I could begin questioning the poor lady so as to understand a little *what* had happened, and *how,* the door opened, and in came Mrs. Furnival, accompanied by the inspector of police, whom, to her astonishment, she had met on entering the house.

The calm manner and precise questions of the well-practised official soon drew a comprehensible statement of facts from not too clear-headed Miss Morton.

This was the story: Mrs. Furnival had the habit of drawing, on the Saturday morning, sufficient cash to pay the rather heavy weekly bills. This cash, amounting to over 30*l.* she invariably deposited in the drawer of an old-fashioned escritoire, standing in her own private room; and the key of this drawer she wore attached to her watchguard, as the money remained from the Saturday till the Monday morning, when she paid it out regularly.

Miss Morton declared that she had seen her put the money in the drawer as usual, lock it, and take the key; she had noticed it particularly, because the whole sum happened to be in very bright gold sovereigns, and it almost filled the small drawer. Miss Morton had then gone to the study, occupying herself with her usual duties, until about six o'clock, when the principal still being absent, she had availed herself of her privilege to use her room; and thither she had gone, and remained till she quitted it to head the tea-table. On her return she had found the room exactly as she left it, and it was only by a mere chance that on passing the escritoire she saw the important drawer open and the money gone. The lock had not been tampered with; there was no sign of any one having entered the room; but every one of the golden sovereigns was gone.

Mrs. Furnival, on her part, said she had certainly locked-up and taken the key, which had remained safely in her possession all day, and that she had not entered the room since.

The lock was very peculiar: it would have been easier to break it than unlock it with any key but its own. It was, however, quite right, and the key turned in it easily as ever.

Inspector S. examined lock, drawer, and room with great minuteness and official silence; then he examined the window and ground beneath, then the servants, and finally the young ladies, with the exception of Myra Richardson and myself, who had been out all day; but, in spite of his acuteness, he could find no clue to the robber.

He came back to Mrs. Furnival's boudoir before he left; and I heard him say in a low tone as he took his leave, "It is someone in the house, I am certain, or who, at any rate, has an accomplice in the house. However, I daresay we shall ferret them out."

Mrs. Furnival dismissed him graciously; but his last words did not tend to smooth the anxious ruffle that had been gathering on her face ever since the investigation of the officer tended only to increase its mystery.

I do not imagine the principal cared so much about her 34*l.* as the inspector thought; she was thinking, perhaps, how damaging it would be to her school if—Well, no matter; her fears, perhaps, made her imaginative.

I had been so engrossed with the thing itself, that I had paid little attention to anyone but the chief actors in it; so when I happened to go back to the library, to fetch the bonnet I had hastily thrown there, I was surprised to find Myra Richardson sitting in exactly the same attitude in which I had left her nearly an hour ago. She did not move even when I entered.

"Are you asleep, Myra?" I exclaimed, flashing the candle across her face; and then I saw that it was ghostly white, though her beautiful eyes were shining like stars.

"Were you frightened?" I said, again holding the candle in front of her.

"I am very thankful we were out of the house," she answered slowly, and apparently with an effort; for her lips trembled.

"You absurd child! Why, who would have suspected us? We are *ladies.*"

"True,' she said softly; "but—" And then she rose and gathered her shawl round her as if she were very cold, and hurried out of the room.

Half-an-hour after, we were all assembled round the supper-table, and, as usual, Myra Richardson was the gayest and loveliest amongst us.

Inspector S. was very clever, very acute; but he did not seem clever enough to ferret out the mystery of the Maldon-Lodge robbery.

A week and then a fortnight passed, and still no clue to the robber had been found, neither had the police been able to throw suspicion on any servants in or about the house.

Mrs. Furnival would have desired it to be thought that the young ladies were above suspicion—for the sake of her school, I suppose; but policemen are not schoolmistresses, and the inspector would ask troublesome questions of the servants, and the servants, too, would speak of them as human beings; and so, in spite of madame's polite letters and polite assurances, more than one lady wrote urging the speedy solution of the mystery or the return home of her daughter.

Mrs. Furnival maneuvred well in the emergency: she melted to tears with the papas; she pleaded her widowhood to the mammas; and to both she whispered mysterious words concerning a suspicion of her own, which, if proved, would satisfy all parties.

I do not know whether this was really true; but during that fortnight I never saw the shadow of a smile on her pale delicate face, and, though she came amongst us as usual, she was strangely reserved.

On the second Sunday after the robbery, I happened to walk home with Mrs. Furnival from evening service. I was a favourite of hers; and as we entered the grounds, she put her arm through mine, and, slackening her pace, said, "It is a lovely evening, Ethel; let us have a turn round the rose-garden."

She had a remarkably delicate face, but I thought it looked very death-like in the clear dusk; she leant heavily on my arm too.

As we entered the beautiful little enclosure, where the rich odour of roses of all kinds came almost oppressively on the evening air, she said suddenly, "Ethel, I want to tell you a secret; you are the only girl I would trust. I have been robbed again!"

I started with almost a scream.

"Hush!" said the principal, "hush! I must have this kept secret."

"Robbed again!" I repeated. "When?"

"Last night. Listen quietly. I did not put the money in the escritoire till ten o'clock in the evening, thinking it safer in my own pocket; but being in a hurry, and tired, and never sleeping with money in my bedroom, I put it in the usual place. This morning, on going to take it out before going to church, I found the drawer empty, unlocked as before."

"Incomprehensible!"

"Someone has a key which opens the drawer, that is evident."

I was silent for a moment, perfectly dumbfounded by the intelligence. At length I said impetuously, "You must have us all searched, Mrs. Furnival; it is only just to the innocent.'

"I can't, Ethel," she replied quickly; "at least, not yet. I have told you this in confidence, remember. You must not betray my secret."

"But—"

At that instant, however, came the sound of a quick light step running along on the other side of the rose-hedge, and startled us both into silence. A very light step it was—light enough for only one pair of feet that we knew; and the next instant Myra Richardson ran by, looking neither to the right nor left, and with her head bent down in a peculiar fashion.

"Myra," whispered Mrs. Furnival. "What is she doing here? Why is she not with the others?"

"Shall I call to her?" I said.

"No, no, not for worlds!" answered the principal in quite a pained tone; and then she took my arm again, and began walking slowly back to the house.

A few of the girls were assembled in the supper-room as we entered, and among them was Myra, standing before the looking-glass decking her hair with lilies of the valley; and I must say I had never seen a lovelier face than that the glass reflected.

"Myra," said Mrs. Furnival suddenly, "were you in the garden just now?"

"Yes; I went for these." And she came quickly, bringing a handful of lilies. "Are they not sweet?" Mrs. Furnival looked earnestly in her face. "I wish you would remember rules, Myra, and be less childish."

She laughed in reply, and, throwing the rest of the flowers over her head, walked back to the looking-glass. She had no veneration, the little Australian, not even for the principal.

We went next into that boudoir which was already held in bad odour, and then, after Mrs. Furnival had carefully closed the door, she sat down-just within reach of the last rays of summer twilight.

"I am suffering from a horrible suspicion," she said. "Ethel, can you guess it?"

"No," I answered stoutly; and in truth I could not.

She looked in my face for a moment, and then, growing stern, said, "Was Myra Richardson with you all that Saturday?"

"Yes," I returned stiffly; for I was so confused that I scarcely knew whether she meant to imply suspicion of me or Myra by the question.

"Most mysterious," muttered Mrs. Furnival, leaning back in her chair wearily; "I—"

But at that moment Miss Morton knocked at the door, and I was obliged to go away; but it was in a very disturbed frame of mind.

I hoped I should have some opportunity of continuing the conversation; but, to my surprise, I was neither summoned again to the boudoir, nor did the principal seek me privately. From that Sunday evening too, though she was kind as ever, I fancied she rather avoided my society.

All this was very perplexing and un-comfortable, and I became very miserable. Naturally I watched suspiciously my school-fellows, more especially Myra; but nothing could I discover which could at all help me to understand Mrs. Furnival's strange conver-sation. The girls were all looking forward to the breaking-up dance, and were much more occupied with toilet-matters than robberies; indeed, I doubted if any one of them but my-self recollected the mysterious robbery at all.

As for Myra, she was gaiety itself in those summer days. The sunshine and heat seemed to madden her with delight, and in spite of every teacher and rule she was not to be lured out of the garden, where she sang with the birds, and basked in the sunshine, and played with the flowers more like some wild nymph of the woods than a young lady of the nine-teenth century, the heiress of Australian gold.

Alas, when I think of those days, even now I exclaim, "Poor Myra!" and shudder. She was so beautiful too, that night of the ball—the fairest of all, and the gayest.

We were all unusually gay too, unusually happy; and even now I seem to see before me the flushed happy faces, and hear the ringing laughter—nay, the very strains of the then fashionable dance music. There are some scenes that stamp themselves indelibly on the memory, why or wherefore we know not. I have been to many a gayer dance than that school-party, many a one I enjoyed more, and yet I think I remember that one more distinctly than any other.

I was just in the midst of a very animated conversation with one of my partners, a tall young man whom I regarded with almost veneration as he rejoiced in the title of captain, when Mrs. Furnival touched me on the shoulder, and said, "Ethel, have you seen Myra?"

I turned sharply round.

"She was my *vis-à-vis* in the last set of lancers," I answered. "She can't be far off. Do you want her, Mrs. Furnival?"

"No—that is, I do not see her in the room, and I do not want her to be wandering about in the grounds now the dew is falling so heavily."

I knew the principal well enough to observe that she did not speak quite naturally; besides, as she spoke she glanced again round the ballroom in a manner strangely anxious.

"I will go and see, if you like," I said. "I am not afraid of the dew; and if Myra is anywhere, she is sure to be in the rose-garden."

I ran off as I spoke, wrapping my opera-cloak round me. The night was clear but damp, and the starlight fell softly over the garden, making no unpleasant lounge for over-heated and imprudent dancers. There were but few, however, and those chiefly on the lawn just in front of the house, so I found the rose-garden quite silent and solitary.

I gave but one quick glance round, and was about to return to the ballroom and my interrupted conversation, when again that peculiarly light step, which had disturbed Mrs. Furnival and myself that Sunday evening, fell on my ear.

Before I saw her, I knew that it was Myra. She came along in the starlight, her satin dress glimmering in an almost ghostly fashion, and with her flower-wreathed head again bent towards the ground. I do not know what prevented me calling to her, but I did not. I allowed her to pass on, whilst I stood watching her in silent wonder.

And then a sudden impulse seized me, whether impelled by some fate, or only actuated by the suspicions which had been so constantly sounded in my ears, I do not know; but instead of returning to the house, I passed out of the rose-garden, and ran quickly down to that part of the grounds where each of us girls was allowed to cultivate a piece of garden as she chose.

It was a long strip of ground, at the top of a high bank, at the bottom of which ran a small but tolerably deep river; not the safest perhaps that could have been selected for our gardening operations; but Mrs. Furnival was fanciful about her grounds, and superintended their cultivation herself with almost artistic taste.

Down this walk, lighted by the clear summer stars, I hastened, till I came to Myra's garden.

It was easily distinguishable from the rest by the profusion of lilies of all sorts which grew there. They were her favourite flower; indeed, she had almost a passion for them, and would tend them with a devotion that made all of us laugh.

I looked eagerly round: what could have taken Myra to her garden at that hour? And then I stooped down and examined it carefully. But nothing remarkable appeared, nothing; and I was just about to give it up and go away, when it struck me some of the lily-roots looked more faded than others. I examined them, and only dimly in that light could I see that here and there one or two of them had apparently been freshly planted.

This looked strange, for it was not the time of year for transplanting, and then, as I touched one, I found I could remove it easily, for it was only laid on the earth to look as if still growing.

My blood rushed dizzily to my brain, for I had a horrible idea—a wild horrible suspicion.

Removing my white glove, I began digging up the soft mould with my hand, and then, not more than a few inches beneath the surface, I came against what I had expected. Yes, there in a little heap lay the golden sovereigns robbed from Mrs. Furnival's private drawer.

I shall never forget the shock of that moment. I got up in horror, as if I had come upon some poisonous serpent, and I exclaimed, "O heaven! O Myra, Myra!" in almost agony; and then, without giving myself time for reflection, I hastily covered the sovereigns up again, replaced the roots, and walked slowly back.

I was very young then, and the fact of being the person to discover such a horrible mystery, and bring an accusation, however just, against one of my own companions, made my blood run cold. How heartily I wished I did not know it—that it had been any other than myself to find out this strange secret!

What should I do?

I was sorely perplexed; and as I walked

back that short distance to the house, my imagination conjured up all sorts of horrors in the way of imprisonment and punishment which this knowledge of mine would bring on my beautiful friend.

I went slowly back to the ballroom, but everything seemed changed; and when I saw Myra's form flying through the dance, I could scarcely believe but that I was labouring under some horrible dream. Mrs. Furnival came up to me as I entered.

"What a time you have been, my dear! Miss Myra has reappeared long ago."

"I know; I met her in the garden," I answered feebly. "

In the garden! She did not tell me that. Who was she with?"

"No one.'

"She certainly is most extraordinary;" and Mrs. Furnival again looked curiously round after Myra's beautiful face, and I turned away.

"No," I thought, "I can't tell yet,—I can't in this scene; and there may be something—"

But I was very glad when that long evening was at length over. Never was I more thankful to see the guests depart one after the other, and at length to stand saying good-night to my schoolfellows.

They would remain talking over the party; but I pleaded headache, and got up to my room. To tell the truth, I was anxious to be there before Myra, for I wanted to think quietly as to what I should do. It was a horrible secret for a young girl to be burdened with, and I could not decide what to do with it. I sat on my bed there, thinking and still perplexed, gradually unfastening my ornaments and ball-dress, when Myra's step approached quietly, and in another instant she entered.

"Then you are not in bed after all, Ethel," she said, throwing herself carelessly on the sofa, and beginning to tear-off her bracelets in her usual impatient fashion.

"What have you been doing?"

"Thinking," I said gravely.

"Thinking! and of what? What Captain Tyler was saying with such *empressement* as he took leave?"

"No, Myra, of something more—more—" And then my courage failed me, and I could say no more; but hurriedly beginning to undress, I threw myself into bed, and drew the curtains, to hide the view of that beautiful figure in white satin which still sat by the toilet-table.

Whether I went to sleep I know not; if I did, my dreams must have been vivid as reality, for I was haunted by the strange secret I had discovered; and at length, sitting up in bed, I drew back the curtains. The moonlight was streaming into the room, and I could distinctly see the form of Myra lying with open eyes, her face turned towards the window.

Some impulse seized me, whether good or bad I know not; but I sprang up, and crossing the room with my bare feet, knelt down by my schoolfellow's bed.

"Hush, Myra," I said, laying my hand upon her arm; "don't speak, don't move. I want to tell you a secret."

"A secret!" she said, in a frightened voice.

"Yes; listen. Down under the lilies in your garden, Myra, lie all Mrs. Furnival's sovereigns."

It seemed as if I were speaking in my sleep; but before me Myra's figure rose slowly, and with a horror that was awfully lifelike. I shall never forget her face; for a moment it worked till it was all distorted; then it calmed down.

"How did you find it out?" she said in a whisper.

"By chance," I answered.

"When?"

"This evening."

"And who have you told? Does Mrs. Furnival know?"

"Not yet."

"And you will tell her?"

"Myra, I must."

She sank back on her pillow and moaned; and I buried my face in the coverlid and began to cry quickly, for that moan was so horrible to hear.

"Why did you do it?" at length I said, clasping hold of the soft white fingers and holding them to my cheek. "O Myra, Myra! why did you do it?"

"I do not know," she answered quickly; and then she turned away her face, and would not speak for all my questions and sobs.

She lay perfectly still, with the moonlight playing on her face; now and then she gasped quickly, and her hands were clenched, but otherwise she seemed to bear the accusation more quietly far than I could make it. At length, however, she roused herself, and pushing back her auburn hair, pressed her hands tightly to her temples.

"You will tell them all to-morrow, I suppose, Ethel, and I shall be sent to prison?"

"I don't think Mrs. Furnival will send you to prison."

Again we were silent; then she said, "Ethel, it is very hard to be burdened with the sins of one's parents; this is a hard world, is it not?"

I had not found it so as yet; and I answered faintly, "I do not know."

Then she laid her hand on my head in a quaint old-fashioned manner, and said, "I am quite sane to-night, Ethel, mind that. When I took that—that gold, I was not perhaps; but to-night I am. I keep my secret too—no one knows, no one knows!" And then she lay back, covered herself up with the sheet, and turned away; and though I knelt by her for nearly an hour, she would say nothing more.

I sobbed a good deal quietly, and then I grew weary, for I was very young, and crept back to my own bed and there fell asleep. It was a long sleep too; for when I woke, the sun was shining in my eyes and it was four o'clock.

I raised myself from the pillow with a dim uneasy consciousness of something wretched having happened, and looked towards Myra's bed. Was I still dreaming, or was the bed really empty? In an instant I was up and feeling with my hands to satisfy my eyes. Myra was gone!

The horror of the moment turned me icy cold, though I stood in the full rays of the early sunshine. I turned to the window; it was open!

I do not know how it was, but in a moment I seemed to understand what had happened, and to take-in all the horrors of the reality. To put on my boots and dressing-gown was the work of a moment, and then climbing out of the window, I let myself fall on to the soft mould beneath. I knew I should see the print of small feet there. Then bareheaded and shivering in the cold morning air, I ran down the garden.

No idea of going to Mrs. Furnival, or alarming any one, entered my head. I went immediately to Myra's garden, and when I was there I turned from the flower-border to the bank, at the foot of which runs the river.

I shall never forget the scene of golden light, white mist, and shiny water, that I there looked on. I seemed to note every detail, though I was looking but for *one object*, with a horror that almost froze me. But no; I could not see it. Thank heaven, it was—I was turning away thinking that, when my eye happened to fall on the flags below

There was something white at the verge— something like a human hand caught in the green weed that grew so thickly just there.

Never shall I forget the horror of that moment. I did not exclaim, I did not utter a sound; but I slid down the bank, and, heedless of danger, entered the water. Up to my knees, then up to the waist, clinging desperately to the rushes; and then, under the water, held down by those entangling weeds, I found what I sought.

Though, with all my strength, I battled to bring her to land, I knew that she was dead—drowned. I knew that she had succeeded; and then my misery burst silence, and, winding my arms round the poor dead form, I uttered wild cries.

There was an inquest, a funeral, and then Myra Richardson disappeared from amongst us. The girl's strange death was talked of as a nine-days' wonder: "temporary insanity" had been the verdict returned, and, for a time, all the odd ways of the poor child were talked of and commented on, and then the mystery was allowed to drop, and she was forgotten. That she was concerned in the mysterious robbery was never known; and no one but Mrs. Furnival ever heard the story of the stolen sovereigns from my lips; and though sometimes the share in the tragedy which I had had made me long to tell it to someone, I felt that, in keeping it secret, I was doing that which the dead girl would most have desired.

It was not till months afterwards that I heard some details of Myra's history, which, perhaps, some might consider explanatory of her strange conduct.

It appears that she was the daughter of a wealthy Australian merchant, who had married a female convict, whose history was scarcely clearer than her daughter's. Though well born and educated, Mrs. Richardson had been convicted of some theft, and, in spite of the evidence that insanity was in the family, and had before exhibited itself under this form, was transported for seven years. At the end of the time, still retaining magnificent beauty, she had won the affections of a rich trader, and married him.

The secret of her mother's disgrace had been kept from Myra for some time; but, by some chance, she came to know of it, and whether insanity was really already in her blood, or her vivacious nature was too strongly impressed with the story, was not known; but from that time the wild elfishness of character took possession of her, and her father, terribly troubled, hoping to mend matters by change of scene and climate, resolved on sending her to England.

Mrs. Furnival had been given some hints of the real state of the case, but not sufficient to guide her in her education of the unfortunate child, or, when her troubles came, to teach her how to act.

Poor beautiful Myra! Terrible indeed must have been the suffering she endured the night before she committed that wild desperate deed; and mad as she may have been in regard to the robbery (for after all she only buried her treasure), I for one never believe that last act was done in a fit of insanity.

The wild Australian had probably made up her mind that her mother's evil fate should never be hers. Still, after all, we can but surmise; for as her last words which sounded in mortal ears declared—no one knew her secret. It was hers and hers alone; and till she rises from her quiet forgotten grave, and tells out the sad story to One who will not judge her harshly, it will remain for ever a buried mystery.

MY AUNT'S PEARL RING

"THAT pearl ring, Mabel,—you prefer that to all the others?"

I fancied my aunt spoke in a slightly regretful tone, although she had emptied the contents of her little jewel-casket into my lap so carelessly, and bid me select the trinket which should be her gift to me on my approaching wedding-day.

"You know I have a strange fancy for pearls, aunt; but if you have the slightest affection for this ring, I would not take it for the world;—and indeed," I added, setting the delicate little circlet aside, and turning again to its more glittering fellows, "I daresay I can find one which pleases me equally amidst such a collection."

But with a little hasty movement my aunt threw it back, saying, "No, no, my dear; if you like it, take it. I have no affection for it. Heaven knows I have little cause ever to wish to see it or hear of it again." And then, seeing that I looked up in some amazement at her unusual energy, she added, with almost a scornful smile, "What are jewels to me now?"

We were silent a moment or two, and somehow I felt that, in spite of the quiet manner with which my still beautiful aunt sank back in her chair and resumed her embroidery, I had inadvertently touched on some painful memory, and roused some emotion which it required all her strength of will to repress.

She was no ordinary character, as I well knew. Self-possessed and reserved to a remarkable degree, she had always inspired me with more awe and respect than loving confidence; but as she sat there, with the evening light falling on her delicate face, her lips firmly compressed, her brows slightly frowning, something seemed suddenly to thaw my heart towards her; and in spite of her frigid manner, I drew closer to her, and, laying my head on her knee, said softly, "I fear I have pained you, aunt Magdalen."

Her needle went very fast for a few stitches, and then, as if with some resolution which cost her an effort to make, she laid down her work, and fixing her eyes on mine, gazed at me for some moments thoughtfully and intently.

"I am not superstitious, Mabel, as you know," she began slowly, and laying her light cold hand on my head; "but I think before we quite conclude the matter of the pearl ring, I should like to tell you its history. I am not sure that you will think it an auspicious bridal gift when you know all about it, and—and me."

Her voice dropped painfully as she said the last words, and I saw by her face that the memory of some past sorrow was pressing upon her with a force that even her strong will could scarcely meet and master.

"It is not a pleasant story to tell, Mabel, and it is one which, though known to others, *my* lips have never before told; and—"

"If it is painful to you, dear aunt," I interrupted quickly, "do not make such an effort for me, then. Never mind about the ring, aunt Magdalen; give me that little cross you used to wear,—indeed the only ornament I have ever seen upon you: I shall treasure it even more than the pearl ring."

"Hush, my dear—hush!" she answered, more kindly, however, than was her wont. "I have made up my mind to tell you this story. Do not interrupt me, but listen quietly; and if you can draw any lesson for your own future guidance in life, do; and then, at any rate, some good may result from my pain.

*

I was very handsome when I was your age, Mabel; I was, moreover, accomplished; and having lived a good deal with a fashionable cousin in London, I had acquired all the polish of manner, at least, which the habitual contact of good society gives. So when on one of my rare visits home I met and became engaged to Lord Rutherford, the possessor of Rutherford Park, no one was very much surprised, except perhaps myself.

Your mother was many years my senior, and though an angel in disposition, she had never been remarkable for beauty; neither was she accomplished; and she therefore regarded me as a marvel, and thought no position too high for me to aspire to. My father shared her enthusiasm, and the consequence was, when I occasionally came to spend a month or two at the quiet country rectory, I was treated as a kind of divinity by my own family, and fêted and admired as a superior being by the quiet country neighbours.

In justice to myself, however, I must say that, although naturally enough I was willing and pleased to be flattered, my head was not altogether turned by it; and I had acquired enough worldly knowledge in my London experiences to know that beauty was not the sole charm by which husbands were to be won—especially noble husbands—or fate ruled. And when, therefore, Lord Rutherford asked me to be his wife I was very much delighted and certainly a little surprised.

I accepted him without a moment's hesitation; or rather, I should say, I accepted his coronet and fortune; for of himself, except as a necessary appendage to these desirable blessings, I thought nothing.

He was dark, and stern, and rather cold in manner; and certainly had he been a simple nobody I should never have dreamed of preferring him to a light-hearted captain of dragoons who happened to be staying in the neighbourhood, and who for some time had been paying me devoted attention.

Guy Deveril was one of those men to whom the term "fascinating" may be truly applied. He certainly thoroughly understood the art of making himself agreeable; and if he did not win hearts quite so quickly or constantly as he fancied, he won without difficulty those first vivid fancies which a little constancy on his part could soon have made firm, even fierce, love.

I certainly liked Guy better than Lord Rutherford, and it was rather a trial at first to have to give him up as my constant companion in walking and riding, and take dark, stern Eustace instead; but the coronet kept me firm for the first few days, and then gradually my betrothed's truly noble character became more revealed, and if I did not love him enthusiastically, I learned to respect and honour him, as well as to appreciate his refined and intellectual conversation.

The more I was with him, too, the higher grew this esteem; and, in justice to myself, I must say, that though I felt my own nature was scarcely fit to soar with his, I made vigorous efforts to make myself more worthy of him.

I was clever after a style of my own, and perhaps really more acute in my appreciation of character than Lord Rutherford, and I clearly saw that he did not comprehend me; I saw that he worshipped rather some ideal standard of female perfection which he imagined developed in me than my real true self.

But this pained me.

In the first place, I was too sincere to wish to deceive him; but at the same time I was afraid of his suddenly becoming aware of my inferiority and ceasing this devoted worship.

In spite of my disquietude, however, the courtship proceeded very quietly for some weeks, and things were advancing satisfactorily towards the consummation of all our hopes. The wedding-day was fixed, my trousseau was nearly ready, the sojourn for the honeymoon was decided on, and as far as human ken could reach nothing appeared which could possibly interfere with the event which was to place a coronet on my brow and make me the wife of dark, stern Eustace Rutherford.

[My aunt paused a moment, and looking dreamily out over the distant scene of orchard and garden, dimly glimmering in the last faint rays of the red sunset, sighed sadly.]

I seem to see those scenes of the past still. I could almost fancy that figure pacing there beneath on the lawn, and pausing every now and then to look at this window, was that of Eustace Rutherford. It was just such an evening, I remember, when as I sat there on that seat, Mabel, over which hangs that rich laburnum, I was startled by Eustace's hurrying up in a breathless state, and seizing my hand, exclaiming, "Magdalen, I must leave you; my mother has been taken dangerously ill and I must go to her. I have only an instant to say good-bye, but I will write;" and then, before I could say a word, he had kissed me hastily and was gone.

I turned pale and cold, though I scarcely knew why, and without further delay I went into the house to tell the news to my sister Alice.

"This is indeed sad. Poor Eustace! he loves his mother so devotedly," she exclaimed simply.

"Yes," I answered; "and it will put off our marriage for Heaven knows how long."

Ah, in my selfishness I was a true prophetess.

Alice looked up gravely. "That should scarcely be your first thought, Magdalen."

"I know it ought not; but I'm not a good young person like you, Ally, and—and besides I'm in love, you know," I replied lightly, as I was wont to do when I felt I ought to be ashamed of myself; and then I sat down to the piano and began dashing off a brilliant waltz, till my sister's light hand laid upon my shoulder suddenly checked me.

"Don't play that now, Magdalen; come to tea and calm yourself a little," she said. "You are unwise to give way to such excitable moods: Lord Rutherford is not the nature to stand it."

"I know that, and I do not indulge in them before him," I replied.

"But if you allow this habit to grow, when you are married you will not find the restraint easy," she exclaimed.

"I shall not trouble myself then; my husband must take me for what I am," was my reply.

I needed not Alice's firm "You are very wrong, Magdalen," to make me aware of the fact; but somehow that evening I felt as if some great pressure had been taken off me, and my own true nature, evil though it might be, would out.

I went out again into the garden, to avoid continuing the conversation, and to calm myself.

The next day I watched anxiously for a letter—for, truth to tell, I was particularly anxious that my wedding should take place at the time named, and if Lady Rutherford died I knew this could not be. But to my surprise Eustace did not write for a couple of days, and then only a hurried note to say his mother continued ill, but that he thought there were still faint hopes of her ultimate recovery: he did not even mention his return.

I was disappointed; but at the same time I knew Lord Rutherford's cold nature, and I therefore comforted myself with the thought that he probably had not the gift of warm love-letter writing. I was naturally of a lively disposition, and putting the epistle in my desk, I certainly troubled myself but little about it, turning my attention to such amusement as Eustace's absence now gave me leisure to join in.

Instead of confining myself to the rectory garden, I went visiting amongst the neighbouring families, and—alas for my weakness and idleness!—again fell into the company of Guy Deveril. Since my engagement to Lord Rutherford I had done my best to avoid Captain Deveril, feeling that it was better for my own happiness and also more pleasant to Eustace, who, though he would not stoop to outward demonstration of jealousy, was one who I knew would brook no rival. Now that I had nothing to do, however, no one to be with constantly, the temptation was too great for me to resist, and, insensibly, from meeting Guy in company, and talking generally with him, I passed on to strolling with him apart from others, and finally to *tête-à-tête* rambles and moonlight saunterings, much in the same free way which I had been wont to indulge in before my betrothal.

Guy was more on a level with myself than the stern intellectual Lord Rutherford, and the effort I made to comprehend and appreciate Eustace was not necessary when I was with the gay captain.

He loved pleasure, romance, poetry, music—all that could give sun shine to life, but which gives no help to weather its storms—and I was of the same light nature. His company charmed me, his flattery charmed me, and that gallant attention in little matters, which Lord Rutherford would never have thought of paying, charmed me. But though I indulged my vanity and love of gaiety, my conscience was still on the alert, and as yet I was faithful in my thoughts to Eustace, and if he had but returned then, as I hoped and expected, all might yet have been well. Ah, how different indeed might my fate have been!

Days, weeks passed—a couple of months went by, and Lord Rutherford only wrote that his mother lingered still, but in such a state that from day to day they expected her to breath her last. Our union he never mentioned; only once or twice did he speak of his return; and though his letters came regularly enough, and always breathed affection, I began to receive them as a matter of course, and to grow slowly less interested in their contents.

I was a little displeased with Eustace at thus deserting me for his dying mother, and the attentions of Guy Deveril were therefore all the more welcome; and, I know not whether by design or not, just at that time Guy pressed them more assiduously than ever, and whenever he could be he was always beside me.

Alice shook her head, and my father looked grave; but I used to laugh and say I was dull without Eustace, and should die if I had no one to help me while away the time, or else I put on an offended air, and with flashing eyes asked them if they distrusted me. My foolish pride made me obstinate—I would not be reprimanded and ruled by simple Alice, who spent her life in cutting-out clothes for the poor, and visiting the sick—and in very bravado I increased rather than diminished my intimacy with the gay captain.

Meanwhile my imprudence was attaining its culminating point.

In a neighbouring town there was a grand fancy fair about to be held in aid of some charity, and a cousin of Guy Deveril, who was one of the lady patronesses, asked me to join her in keeping a stall. The invitation was sent to me through Guy, and he was very urgent that I should accept it, as the office of driving me to and from Little Denton would fall to him, and indeed we should be able to pass the day together in a scene of excitement and gaiety such as we both loved.

My conscience was not quite easy, but I agreed, and set about preparing a dress which should do justice to the occasion and my own beauty; and after not a few hours' hard labour I laid a costume out before Alice's wondering eyes which even she declared would make me the belle of the fête.

You will think me very foolish, Mabel; but do you know I dreamt of that dress? I longed to wear it as eagerly as any village school girl longs to put on her new bonnet. You may conceive, then, my disappointment when, on the eve of the fair, I received a letter from Eustace, which at first sight seemed to make the pleasure impossible. It was a long letter, filled with accounts of his mother's health, and his own intense anxiety to get over the next few days, during which a crisis was expected to take place in the disease; but in a short post script he said, "I have heard that you have been asked to patronise the charity fair at Little Denton. I will send you 10*l*. as my contribution. Of course under our present circumstances you cannot be expected to appear at such a place."

That was all. He seemed to consider it a matter of course that whilst his mother lay dying I should never dream of appearing in any public place of amusement. To make such a request as a favour granted to himself would have appeared like an insult to my good feeling and good taste.

But instead of arguing in this way, I exclaimed, "How selfish lovers are! Eustace expects me to feel as much for his mother, whom I never saw in my life, just because she is his mother, as he does! Absurd!" And then crumpling up the letter, I dashed downstairs to stop Guy Deveril, who happened at that moment to be passing the garden-gate and casting longing looks up at my window, to tell him that after all I must give up the anticipated pleasure; and also to ask him to make my excuses to his cousin for deserting her party after so short a notice.

"Give up the fair!" exclaimed Captain Deveril. "Why, Magdalen, whatever spirit of change has seized on you?"

"It is a great disappointment," I said; "but Lord Rutherford would be seriously offended, I fear, if I went."

Guy never spoke against Eustace to me; but he was always meaningly silent whenever his name was mentioned.

"And what harm can you do his lordship by going? By George, a man should not leave a girl for ten or twelve weeks in such an inexplicable manner, and then expect her to live like a nun! Rutherford is unreasonable!"

I was silent, for I did not choose to join Guy in abusing my betrothed.

"I suppose he thinks it would look odd," I said after a pause; "and perhaps it would; but I am very sorry. Will you tell Mrs. Deveril, and say also that Lord Rutherford intends contributing 10*l.* to the charity?"

"Let him keep his money!" exclaimed Guy savagely. "10*l.* won't make up for your absence; and indeed, Magdalen, I must say I think you are a little ridiculous."

"Ridiculous, Captain Deveril! Why, what can I do? I would do anything to go—at least," I added as Guy turned suddenly and looked at me with a strange expression—an expression which frightened me a little—"anything that was not absolutely wrong."

"Well, then, burn Lord Rutherford's letter, and *go*," was his reply in low tones. "Perhaps it would not be quite the correct thing, all things considered, for you to attend the stall and make yourself conspicuous; but there would be no manner of harm in your driving quietly over and walking through the place with the other steady people who come to spend their money. Even Lord Rutherford only meant your joining the stall-keepers. Besides, Magdalen, the Little Dentonians are a distinct set from this neighbourhood. Few persons would recognise you."

He was leaning over the gate, and some-how his hand touched mine as he said this; but I did not remove mine.

"It will be horribly dull without you, Magdalen; and go I must, for I have promised Julia," he went on. "Do come. There really won't be any harm."

Still I hesitated. I was sorely tempted. I thought of the elegant dress, the pleasures of a day leaning on Guy's arm in a tolerable crowd of company; and then I contrasted the drear-iness of twelve whole long hours wandering about the dull garden or village, and Guy at Little Denton. Surely Eustace did expect too much; besides, would he ever know?

"Come," Guy exclaimed suddenly. "You relent. You won't begin slavery till you leave the altar, at any rate; and I shall be at the gate to-morrow punctually at twelve. Good-night." Without waiting for me to say yes or no, the captain turned as he spoke, and disappeared behind the rose-hedge.

When I went into the house ten minutes after, I never said a word to Alice about Lord Rutherford's letter; and when she said to me, "I suppose, Maggy, you are quite ready for to-morrow," I answered simply, "Yes; quite."

Well, Mabel, I went to that fête, and I confess I enjoyed it. My disposition was one which thoroughly loved excitement; and whilst flattery and compliments sounded in my ears conscience had no chance of being heard. I was the handsomest girl there; and Guy, proud of being my chosen cavalier, was as devoted as I could possibly desire. Indeed that day he ventured on more downright love-making than he had ever before attempted; and he gave me to understand (at least so I thought) that even then, if I would desert Eustace Rutherford, he would only too readily claim me as a wife. I came home in a whirl of excitement; and it was only when I laid my head on my pillow, weary and exhausted, that my restless thoughts turned to consider what might be the consequences of my conduct.

I grew strangely anxious now that I had dared fate; and I trusted most intensely that Lord Rutherford would remain away from the park long enough for the excitement of the fair to subside entirely. So anxious was I, that I condescended to say to Alice that I thought perhaps I had outstepped the bounds of propriety in going, and that I hoped she would not mention it in Eustace's presence.

It happened that on the previous day I had lost a small locket, of no great value; but being particularly fond of it (and indeed of all jewelry), I had shown some vexation at the loss, and sought anxiously about; and the next day I was not surprised therefore to see Guy appear at a later hour than usual, as he had promised to go to Denton and make inquiries.

I was seated in my accustomed place under the drooping willow, working, when Guy approached, and throwing a small packet into my lap, dropped into the seat beside me. "My locket! " I exclaimed. "A thousand thanks! I scarcely expected you would succeed."

"Nor have I," replied Guy. "I thought that, however, might replace it. I went to Smith's, but they had nothing like the locket; and I knew your fancy for pearls."

Meanwhile, in some surprise, I had unfastened the packet, and discovered a magnificent pearl ring instead of my humble little gold medallion.

"O, but, Guy, I ought not to accept it!" I exclaimed. "You forget I am engaged to Lord Rutherford."

"Stuff! Are you never going to take a friendly gift from anyone when you are his wife? Nonsense, Magdalen! I was the means of your losing your pet locket, and I do my best to replace it. Do not be so unkind as to reject my offering."

A little while ago I should have refused it firmly; but the wrong path descends very easily, though swiftly, and I was already some way in my descent. "Eustace must never know about it, then," I thought; but I slipped on the beautiful trinket, and laughed as Guy declared I ought only to wear pearls, for they were the only ornament delicate enough for my fragile white fingers. Still I was not quite easy; and when Alice suddenly joined us, I carefully hid the hand newly decorated from her sight.

I do not think Guy was pleased at this interruption; but for once Alice was not to be frightened away by even Guy's displeasure, and producing her work, she sat down and remained with us till the captain reluctantly said he must prepare for his walk home; and even whilst we sauntered down to the gate, and stood for an instant or two chatting, she remained within view on the lawn, as if resolutely determined to watch him out and me in.

But I was not inclined for a lecture; and so leaning my arms on the gate, I resolved to try Alice's patience a little.

Presently a step coming in the direction Guy had gone made me look up. Of course it must be Captain Deveril returning for something. I saw a man's shadow approaching, and then I started back. It was Lord Rutherford who stood before me.

I turned icily cold as he caught me in his arms.

"How you startle me! I did not expect you in the least," I exclaimed; and making an effort to hide my embarrassment under a show, at least, of delight,—"When did you come? How is Lady Rutherford? Why did you not write?"

"Not a dozen questions, please, dearest, in one breath," he answered, with a pleased laugh, however. "Let me look at you, and see that it is truly yourself."

He was in high, even excited spirits for him; and I could not help gazing up at him in astonishment, remembering his late anxious letters.

He rushed into the house to give Alice and my father a hasty greeting, and then rejoined me in the garden, having, he said, something particular to say to me. My guilty conscience would have shrunk had he not uttered the words so joyfully, and seemed so happy; and so I stood there waiting for him, and most earnestly trusting that all would be right.

A favourable turn had taken place in his mother's malady, and now the physicians ordered an immediate removal abroad; and her great desire was that our marriage should take place immediately, and that after a short honeymoon we should join her in Italy. Lord Rutherford urged me most earnestly to accede to her wish and his, and of course I was willing enough.

Eustace talked unusually fast; there was much to arrange and little time to do it in, as the wedding would have to take place early in the ensuing week. His own business at the park, too, required his presence; and so after an hour's earnest conversation he prepared to leave me. I could scarcely believe, as I walked down to the gate the second time that evening, that in such a short space so much had happened. Guy was almost forgotten— the fair quite. All I remembered was that next Tuesday the ambition of my life would be gratified, and I should belong to the British peerage.

We stood at the gate, and for once Eustace lingered and we talked. I had a nervous habit of twisting my fingers when excited; and was it my evil fortune or an avenging Nemesis made me fidget with them then? My thoughts were so entirely engrossed, that I quite started when Lord Rutherford suddenly exclaimed, "Mind, Magdalen; you have dropped a ring." He stooped, and, to my horror, took up the pearl circlet. "Ah, that reminds me I have forgotten the case of pearls my mother sent you.

What a delicate little affair! I didn't give you this, did I?"

"No," I replied faintly; and then, as he still held it admiringly, I added daringly, "Papa gave it me years ago."

Perfectly satisfied, he slipped it on my finger, saying, "I wish I had remembered my mother's gift. Well, never mind; all will soon be yours. Good-night, dearest."

I had never told Eustace a flat untruth before, though I had not hesitated to deceive him; and I felt anything but comfortable as I retired to bed that night. I was very much excited; nevertheless I could not help being haunted by an uncomfortable dread of to-morrow, and directly I got to my room I carefully locked up that fatal ring.

I was not surprised that the whole of the next day passed without Eustace making his appearance, for I knew he was very busy with servants and tenants; but as the evening drew on I grew a little uneasy.

This uneasiness increased when, just as we were going to sit down to tea, my father suddenly summoned Alice out of the room.

Had anything occurred? My heart beat so that I could hear it above the ticking of the clock.

A quarter of an hour passed, and then, to my intense relief, the door opened, and Alice returned. She was deadly pale, and coming up to me, she seized my hands, and almost dropped down on the stool before me.

"Something has happened?" I exclaimed calmly, for I felt desperate,—"something has happened, Alice? do not keep me in suspense. It is about Eustace?"

"It is," she answered faintly. "O, Magdalen, what have you done?"

"I have been foolish, I know; but—"

"Worse, worse!" she exclaimed. "You have been mad. You have given room for Guy Deveril's boasting."

I turned pale.

"What do you mean, Alice? tell me out plainly what has occurred."

"I scarcely know the whole of the story myself; but it appears that some chance brought Lord Rutherford and Captain Deveril together late last night in company, where it angered Eustace to hear Guy speak of you with the freedom he did. He boasted, Magdalen, that he had more influence over you than your betrothed, and that it was the coronet alone which made you accept Rutherford. Finally, as words got higher, he declared that you wore his gage d'amour on the same finger with that of your engaged ring. Lord Rutherford gave him a flat contradiction, declaring it was false; and you may guess the rest."

"A challenge!" I whispered faintly. And Alice burst into tears.

I cannot distinctly remember all that passed that miserable evening. I was like one in some terrible dream. Somehow I found myself out in the night-air, running between the rose-hedges, and I distinctly see the scene, even now, of summer stars gleaming here and there through the foliage of the trees. And then I stood in the great library of Rutherford House.

Lord Rutherford was sitting by the table, with the light falling on his face, writing; but as I entered he looked up. What I said I know not,—whether I made a full confession and besought pardon, or whether I gasped out a few accusing sentences, and left Eustace to guess the truth, I never distinctly knew. Some words of his, though, stamped themselves on my heart, and haunted me for years:

"Tell me one thing, Magdalen," he said sternly,—"that ring, was it Captain Deveril's gift?"

"Yes," I answered faintly.

"Then you told me a falsehood; *you*, Magdalen, stooped to the degradation of untruth. I have indeed been deceived."

There was a silence—a deadly silence—during which Eustace Rutherford stood looking down on me from his tall height with an expression of stern resolution. I knew I was condemned; my judge was just but merciless.

"I will grant your request," at length he said in clear low tones; "I will apologise to Captain Deveril: he spoke truth;" and then he turned and walked out of the room, and left me.

I never saw him again—indeed never. I was very ill after that, and it was weeks before I recovered complete consciousness, or could comprehend the few lines of farewell he had left for me before starting for the Continent. He did not reproach me for the past, but he only said that we ought both to feel thankful that *before*, rather than *after*, marriage we had discovered how totally unsuited we were to make each other's happiness.

Guy Deveril left the neighbourhood during my illness. You see, Mabel, my punishment was not undeserved; but it was heavy. And now what say you to the pearl ring? Think you that it is an auspicious bridal gift?

A PARTIAL LIST OF SNUGGLY BOOKS

www.ingramcontent.com/pod-product-compliance
Lightning Source LLC
Chambersburg PA
CBHW050405110726
47899CB00008B/2662